THE SOUTHCOTT JEWELS

TRACY GRANT

For Lescaut, who inspired Berowne. And for Cordelia, Suzanne, Malcolm, Cherry Suzette, and Julien, who help keep the inspiration going.

DRAMATIS PERSONAE

*indicates real historical figures

The Rannoch Family & Household

Malcolm Rannoch, MP and former British intelligence agent
Mélanie Suzanne Rannoch, his wife, playwright and former French intelligence agent
Colin Rannoch, their son
Jessica Rannoch, their daughter
Berowne, their cat

Laura O'Roarke, Colin and Jessica's former governess
Raoul O'Roarke, her husband, Mélanie's former spymaster, and Malcolm's father
Lady Emily Fitzwalter, Laura's daughter from her first marriage
Clara O'Roarke, Laura and Raoul's daughter

The Mallinson Family

Julien (Arthur) Mallinson, Earl Carfax, former agent for hire

Katelina (Kitty) Velasquez Mallinson, Countess Carfax, his wife,
former British and Spanish intelligence agent
Leo Ashford, her son
Timothy Ashford, her son
Guenevere (Genny) Ashford, Kitty and Julien's daughter

Hubert Mallinson, spymaster, Julien's uncle
Amelia Mallinson, his wife

David Mallinson, MP, their son
Simon Tanner, playwright, his lover

The Davenport Family & Household

Lady Cordelia Davenport, classicist
Colonel Harry Davenport, her husband, classicist, and former
British intelligence agent
Livia Davenport, their daughter
Drusilla Davenport, their daughter
Cleo, their dog

The Southcott Family

Anthony (Tony) Southcott, Duke of Bamford
Désirée Clairineau, his mistress
Sophie, their daughter
Belle, Sophie's puppy

Prince Franz Stroheim, Austrian diplomat, Désirée's nephew

Henrietta (Hetty) Southcott, Duchess of Bamford
John Wilcox, steward, her lover

Viscount St. Ives, the Bamfords' son

Sylvie, Viscountess St. Ives, his wife

Lady Frederica Rawdon, the Bamfords' eldest daughter
Percy Rawdon, her husband

Helena Ludgrove, the Bamfords' second daughter
Toby Ludgrove, her husband

Rosalind, Condessa Azevado, the Bamfords' youngest daughter
Gaspar, Conde Azevado, Portuguese diplomat, her husband

Mrs. Worthing, housekeeper
Alfred Higgins, footman

The Varon Family

Henriette Varon, former seamstress to Josephine Bonaparte
Lisette Varon, agent, her elder daughter
Minette Varon, her younger daughter

Ill met by moonlight…

—Shakespeare, *A Midsummer Night's Dream,* Act II, scene i

Ill met by moonlight…

    —Shakespeare, *A Midsummer Night's Dream,* Act II, scene i

CHAPTER 1

June 1821
Sawden Park, Surrey

"It's a country house party," Tony said. "We host them all the time."

Désirée folded her arms and regarded the man standing across from her in the blue and gold room she now knew was called the large salon. Anthony Sebastian Aloysius Southcott. Who would always be Tony to her. But who was still, indisputably, the Duke of Bamford. And always would be. "You host them all the time. This isn't my world."

"Since when have you not been at home in any world you chose to make your own?"

Désirée glanced at the guest list on the ormolu table between them. "Since when have the beau monde been so easy to navigate?"

"You could navigate any world you wanted to."

She twitched the list straight on the gilded wood. "Who says I want to navigate this one?"

"Ah." He gave a sweet smile. "There's the rub. There's no reason for you to do so."

Désirée tilted her head to one side. The afternoon light slanting through the French windows lit Tony's eyes. "No reason except that I love you."

Something leapt in his gaze. Those still weren't words either of them said easily, for all they'd accepted them for at least the past six years. "I'd hardly suggest that was a reason for anything."

"You might not. That doesn't mean it isn't."

Tony's gaze settled on her face, suddenly gone serious in that way it could. "Désirée—I'd never ask you to change yourself for me."

"I know it." She reached out a hand and touched his face. "That's one of the reasons I love you. Of course, as your mistress, I'm always going to be on the sidelines."

Tony coughed. "That's part of why Hetty suggested the house party."

Désirée frowned. Usually she could follow Tony's leaps of thought. "Your wife suggested the house party because I'm on the sidelines?"

"Er—no." Tony seemed to be having trouble getting the words out. "She thought—she's said—with the children all settled, she told me she's not opposed to a divorce."

Désirée went still. She'd been an agent for over two decades. She'd been through Napoleon's rise and fall, the Congress of Vienna, Waterloo, the White Terror after Waterloo. Few words could surprise her. But—"A divorce. In the House of Lords."

Tony's gaze shifted to the side. "That's where the bill would have to be heard."

"So she can marry John Wilcox."

Tony shifted his weight from one foot to the other. "She's indicated she would like that. And so that you and I could—"

Désirée stared at her lover. The crinkles round his eyes and the brackets beside his mouth were deeper than when they'd met.

His blond hair was half gray. But the gleam of his blue eyes and the glint of his smile were those of the man she'd met decades ago. Over twenty years. Countless betrayals. Commitments that could never quite be voiced. And yet—

Tony dragged his gaze back to her face. "It seems absurd to go down on one knee when we don't know if it's a possibility. But if I were free, would you do me the honor of becoming my wife?"

Something in his gaze shot straight to her core. In a way that made her defenses slam into place. "You mean the Duchess of Bamford."

"Any woman married to me would be styled the Duchess of Bamford. But even married we're going to be social outcasts."

Désirée tilted her head back to regard her opponent of two decades. "Are you using that to talk me round?"

"I'm rather painfully aware I may have to use every effort at my disposal." He hesitated. His gaze slid to the gilded French windows, which gave onto the terrace and lawn beyond. Where a small girl ran, chasing a puppy, blonde hair and white skirts and pink sash streaming behind her. "Sophie would still have been born before we were married. But it would make her position more secure. And before you rant, I don't think much of a system that lets me be my daughter's stepfather but not her legal father. But that's the world Sophie was born into, and however we work to change it, we have to acknowledge the reality now. That's the reality Sophie has to cope with."

"I won't argue with you there." Désirée held him with her gaze. "Did you say 'we' work to change it?"

"Did I ever say I was against change?" Tony countered. "And I freely admit you've broadened my horizons." He put out a hand, touched her shoulder, dropped it to his side. "It would make our lives easier. And Sophie's. And if we ever—"

"We ever had more children?" The thought should have been more of a shock to voice than it was. She hadn't consciously considered it. Not precisely. But she couldn't say it was an alien idea. "Do you want more children?"

Tony flushed. "That's a question for you."

"It would take both of us, my dear."

"But I'd never ask—but we weren't planning to have Sophie."

"A point." Désirée watched their daughter scoop up Belle, her puppy, and hug her close to her face. She'd enjoy being a big sister. "Perhaps one of the biggest disruptions of my life. But I can't say I'm sorry, and I can't say I'm definitely averse to having more. So you're saying it will make our child or children's lives easier if I marry you, but I don't have to worry about being Duchess of Bamford?"

"You can't avoid the title, but you can ignore it entirely if you choose."

"Obliging of you."

"Or not. Like many things, you can make of it what you will. You've always been good at doing that."

Désirée glanced up at the coffered ceiling and gilt Italian chandelier. And then back at her lover. Why the hell did it matter? Fairy tales that had made more of an impact than she'd ever have acknowledged? Novels and plays? The ridiculously happy examples of some of their friends? "I don't give a damn about being Duchess of Bamford, Tony. Scandal or no. You know my opinion of titles. But I confess I quite like the idea of being your wife."

Something leapt in his eyes. "You mean—"

"If you were free." Her voice was steady but her nerves felt stripped raw. Had she really said it? "And if it were Hetty's choice. I'm not going to deprive another woman of her position."

Tony's gaze locked on her face. His eyes were lit with irony, but wonder lurked at the back. "A position for which you have no use."

"Yes, but that doesn't mean it doesn't matter to Hetty."

"It did matter. I don't think it does now. In any case, I think she wants to be free to marry Wilcox."

The world swam for a moment. Possibilities. The same ones that had teased her after Waterloo. Marriage officially meant less than the commitment to stay together and raise their child that they had made then. Still— "If Hetty wants to marry John, I certainly don't want to stand in their way."

"I certainly won't stand in Hetty's way if she wants a divorce." Tony watched her for a moment. "That doesn't mean you have to marry me."

Désirée put her hands on his chest. "I told you, Tony. Call me sentimental, but I quite like the idea of marrying you."

He put his hands over her own. "My dear." His voice sounded thick.

She squeezed his fingers. Her own voice seemed to be bottled up in her chest. Like it was stuck with cotton wool. "Well then."

Tony pressed his forehead against her own. For a long moment neither of them spoke. Some things really couldn't be put into words. And they would neither of them be able to live down cheap sentiment.

"So Hetty and John are coming to discuss this?" she said at last, drawing back enough to look him in the eye.

"I don't think there's a great deal to discuss." Tony's voice was still thick. "But we do need to explain."

"To—"

"The children."

Désirée took a step back. "You've invited all your children and their spouses and their children to stay with us for the first time so you and Hetty can tell them you're getting a divorce?"

"Er—yes."

This was not the first time she'd confronted an improbable plan from Tony. Though most had involved daring rescues or stealing codes. And many of them she'd been working against. "And you thought it would be better to have a house party, because you like theatrics? I suppose it might give Mélanie Rannoch fodder for her next play."

"There's something to be said for thinking social conventions will quiet things. Though there's no real reason for any of them to mind."

"My dear. Not having a real reason has never made anyone not mind."

"They're all adults." Tony frowned. "At least—"

"Quite."

"You needn't deal with it. It's Hetty's and my problem." His frown deepened. "Perhaps we should tell them without you and Wilcox."

"No, darling." She tightened her fingers over his own. "It is my problem. And John's. We're going to be their stepparents."

Tony's gaze fastened on her face. "Who are you and what happened to Désirée?"

"Just because I didn't see myself having a family until comparatively recently doesn't mean I don't understand what it means. Married or not, we're a family now. We have been, at least since Waterloo. That extends beyond you, me, and Sophie."

His gaze slid over her face, as though searching for something.

"What?" she asked.

"You're remarkable."

"And?"

"Does there need to be an and?"

"I sensed it. And there usually is—it keeps things interesting."

His gaze stayed steady on her face, lit with wry amusement. "I have a vivid memory of your telling me that when you were at your most seemingly disarming, you were at your most lethal."

"I don't remember saying that in particular, but I imagine I did. It was true. And I thought it only fair to warn you."

"Which wasn't precisely lethal of you."

"Perhaps not. Perhaps I was trying to protect myself against your romantic impulses. Against my own reaction to your romantic impulses. But it was quite true that when we met I was lethal and perfectly capable of turning on just about anyone.

That's not what I'm doing now. But of course if that is what I were doing, that's precisely what I'd say." She tilted her head to one side. Her side curls slithered over her shoulder. She had taken to pinning her hair loosely in the country. At the cottage in Normandy she'd often worn it loose entirely. "There's a lot we haven't talked about. A lot from the past. A lot you don't know."

"No." He took a step towards her, still gripping her hands. "The past stays in the past."

"My love. We can't forget it."

"No. But we can say it's not relevant to who we are today."

"It's made us who we are today."

"But it needn't define us now. Those are yesterday's battles. There's no sensing arguing over who betrayed whom or who outwitted whom. It's done. We've survived it. If there's more to know, I don't need to hear it. You're far too generous to let me know about some occasion you pulled the wool over my eyes just for the sake of driving home that you're cleverer than I am. We both know you are."

"I don't know that we know anything of the sort. But I do agree trying to score points over the past is unworthy of both of us. Still, at times one thinks back."

"And I know you're far too pragmatic to waste a second indulging in guilt over the past."

"We can agree to keep quiet. It won't stop either of us possibly learning of something the other did elsewhere."

"And if we do, we'll accept it's in the past."

Désirée looked into his eyes. A thousand moments played through her memory. Moments she knew she had hurt him. Even more moments she'd known it would hurt him if he knew the truth. "Sometimes easier said than done."

"We'll have to trust that we can do it."

"This is all about trust, Tony."

"I've always trusted you."

"Yes, I warned you not to." She reached up and smoothed his hair off his forehead. "My poor fool."

He slid a hand behind her neck. "And yet I wasn't wrong to do so."

She smiled. "We all wear masks, Tony. I was at great pains, for a very long time, not to let you see how well you saw behind mine."

CHAPTER 2

19 June 1815
Brussels

*H*is face was in shadow, but she could see the days-old shadow of beard, the hollows beneath his eyes, the smears of dirt. Blood too. She couldn't tell if it was his own.

"I'm sorry," he said. "I wanted to come at once."

She stepped forwards and wrapped her arms round him. She could breathe again. For the first time since she'd said goodbye to him at the Duchess of Richmond's ball. An unbearable four days ago. "Thank you."

His arms closed round her. They were shaking. She could feel the vibration through the sweat-soaked muslin of her gown. "You have little enough to thank me for. I'm surprised you aren't ranting."

"You're a brilliant man, Tony, but single-handedly defeating the French army is a bit much even for you. And you came back. That's what I wanted more than anything."

His gaze slid over her, taking in the stains on her gown. "You've been—"

"Winding bandages and helping with the wounded. I needed to be doing something. God knows there've been enough wounded on all sides to keep everyone in Brussels busy."

He drew back, gaze dipping to her stomach. "Are you—"

"The baby's fine, Tony. I may not be a girl in the first blush of youth, but I'm perfectly healthy."

He touched her face. "You must have lost—"

Tears she hadn't been able to let herself shed yet clogged her throat. "Yes. I've had reports. And you must have as well."

He nodded. Echoes of what he'd seen on the battlefield were in his eyes. She'd seen enough tending the wounded in Brussels— French, English, Dutch-Belgian, Prussian—to guess. He pressed his forehead against her own. For a moment they stood together in silence.

"It's not safe," he said, into her hair. "The Royalists are going to be drunk with victory. You need to get out of Brussels. And not go back to Paris. I can get you travel papers."

She turned her head against his shoulder but didn't protest. She'd known she had to leave the moment she got the news from Waterloo. She'd only been waiting to see him. "I'm going to Normandy."

"The cottage?"

"The place one's been happiest seems a good refuge."

He tucked her hair behind her ear. "I'll join you as soon as I can."

"Tony—" Fevered promises in the moonlight with a waltz playing and a call to arms sounding seemed different in the cold light of a battle. A battle that had upended everything they both knew.

His fingers trembled against her cheek. "That's what matters now. What we have together. Blame me for the outcome of the battle if you will. But don't push me away. I want to be with you and our child. And I think you want that as well."

"Damn you, you're right. But it's easier for me to walk away than you. That's the thing about defeat."

"I can't walk away immediately. But I can carve out time for myself." He grinned. "At times, it's helpful to be a duke."

"At times?"

"All right, it's usually helpful. And I'd be delighted to argue the negatives of inherited privilege with you. In the cottage in Normandy, where we're going to wait for the birth of our child."

Something leapt within her. Something she wasn't prepared to contemplate at present. "We're not living in a fairy tale, Tony."

"No, we're living in a complicated reality. And we're both adults. Who can work out ways to be happy in that reality."

"Don't you think that's asking a lot?"

"Désirée—" He drew a breath that cut the air between them. "If I could, I'd—"

"What?"

He scraped a hand over his hair. "Isn't it obvious?" The words seemed to be dragged from him, and yet for a moment she had an absurd sense he wanted to get down on one knee. "If I could, I'd ask you to marry me, and we'd be an official family."

She laughed. "Oh, Tony. I'm hardly Duchess of Bamford material. Even if I believed in marriage."

"It's not about that."

"What is it about then?"

"I'm committed. To you. And to the child."

"Well. That's different. We don't need an old-fashioned marriage tie for that."

His hands settled on her arms. "So believe me. I'll be there. Not for a few days or even a few weeks. As much as I can. For the rest of our lives."

Her impulse was to fling her arms round him, but practicality asserted itself. "People will wonder."

"About?"

"Where I've gone. Where you are. There's gossip about us."

"Yes. I know." His brows drew together. "I didn't worry as much before. It didn't seem as troubling if people were worried about me. But if you don't have your country's protection and people are looking for you—"

"They'll look for us together."

"Unless they believe we aren't together. You've threatened often enough to cut me loose. What if you did?"

"I don't think you'd be very happy. I don't think I'd be."

"But what if people thought you had?"

She held his gaze for a moment. For an impossible romantic, Tony was also a brilliant strategist. "An excellent cover story."

"My thoughts exactly."

"You want us to stage a quarrel?"

"No. I want you to disappear as soon as possible. Brussels isn't safe for you, and you're too clever to quarrel with me in public. I'll play the broken-hearted disillusioned lover. I've always worn my heart on my sleeve too much when it comes to our relationship. If I can convince people you've thrown me over, they won't worry where I am when I spend months in Normandy."

"Months?" There was no way she was going to let him know how delightful that sounded.

"Easy enough to disappear on a mission. Easy enough to give everyone a different idea of where I am."

"You have responsibilities." Delicacy forbade her from putting it more into words than that. How odd that she could be delicate.

"My marriage is a ton marriage. Which is to say, a marriage in name only. My wife has her own concerns, and though she's too well-bred to admit it, I think we both know she's happier when I'm not there to interfere. My estates are managed by an excellent steward. My children would far prefer not to have me looking over their shoulders. Which I'll still manage to do far more often than they would like."

"You have a way of making the most complicated things sound absurdly simple, Tony."

"It's nothing of the sort." He took her face between his hands. "I was on the edges of the battle. But I looked into hell. On both sides. I hope to never see anything like that again. Wellington said much the same, and he's far more confident in the rightness of his victory than I am. However we got to this point, surely it tells us we have to grasp hold of what we can. If there was one thing I could hold on to with blood and screams and death all round me, it was you. Wanting to get back to you. Wanting to have a life with you and our child. Not the past, but the future." His fingers trembled against her skin. "You haven't asked, but there hasn't been anyone else. Not for a long time. Not since we were together, actually."

Tony was a romantic, but that caught her by surprise. "We were apart for—"

"Months, sometimes. I never made a decision. Not consciously. It simply didn't seem right. I don't think I'd have had the guts to tell you that until now."

She pressed her cheek against his hand. "Faint heart. I can't say the same. I'm sorry."

"I never asked—"

"Though my past isn't nearly as elaborate as most make it sound. And I can say that in my future, I don't see any need for such adventures."

"I thought you didn't believe in fidelity."

"I don't believe in convention. Which is a rather different thing. I do believe in holding true to what I have. And in being true to myself. Which, at the risk of a dreadful cliché, I think may mean being true to you."

He pulled her to him and kissed her, and then drew back, holding her gaze with his own, while he still cradled her face in his hands. "I'm not particularly proud of what I've made of myself. I was served life on a gilded platter—with sterling beneath the gilding—and I can't claim to have put it to good use. I can't claim to O'Roarke's ideals. I cringe more often than not looking at those I've served. I just went through carnage and looked into hell and wondered what on earth the past two decades had been about. But whatever of me survived that, whatever's left—such as I am, I'm yours, my darling. For the rest of my life."

CHAPTER 3

June 1821
Berkeley Square, London

*M*élanie Rannoch scanned the Berkeley Square Garden. The gnarled trunks of the plane tree, the leafy branches creating a canopy overhead, the gravel walks. The faint rumble of carriage wheels from the square. Her son Colin and daughter Jessica racing between the trees in a game of tag with Emily and Clara O'Roarke and their father Raoul. Who had been knifed just a street away only weeks ago and had almost died on the paving stones.

She looked from side to side, every sense alert. "I can't help wondering."

"What?" Her husband Malcolm came up behind her and slid his arms round her over the back of the bench.

She leant against him, still taking in every detail of the surroundings. The gaps between the branches, the shadows in the streets round the square, the rumble of carriages, the scent of grass and horses carried on the breeze. "Where the next danger will come from."

"Sweetheart." He pressed his chin against her shoulder. "We're in Berkeley Square. In front of our house. With our family."

"Not much more than a stone's throw from where Raoul was attacked."

The children and Raoul were playing catch now. Raoul was helping two-year-old Clara throw a ball. Mélanie scanned the peaceful garden. Always a refuge for their family, but still enough places to hide an enemy. "Raoul almost died. And then you put yourself at risk." She could still feel the churning fear of those hours, waiting to see if the blood their doctor friend Geoffrey Blackwell had transferred from Malcolm to Raoul would save Raoul, and if Malcolm would recover without infection. "And just because Raoul's stepped back from the front lines of danger doesn't mean the danger will leave him alone."

Malcolm pressed a kiss to the top of her head. "You're a former agent, sweetheart."

"I'm never going to be a former anything, darling. But I think we've learnt to our cost how dangerous it is to ignore risks." Her fingers tightened on the metal of the bench. "I'll never forgive myself for—"

"What?"

The bench cut into her palms. "Not being there when Raoul was attacked."

"Mélanie." Malcolm gripped her shoulders and leant over the bench to turn his face to her own. "You couldn't possibly have known—"

"That's just it. We knew he was at risk. He should have had backup."

Her own qualms shot through Malcolm's gaze, inches from her own. "That's on me. You couldn't have—"

"But I could. I know street fights. Better than any of us but Julien, probably." She glanced at Raoul, swinging Jessica up in the air. "He's always so confident he can take care of himself, and we let ourselves be convinced it was all right. I was behaving like a Mayfair lady."

"My darling. You aren't a Mayfair lady."

"Don't I know it."

"That's not what I meant, sweetheart. You could be anything you want. But you haven't forgot who you are."

"That's just it, Malcolm. I did. In the old days I'd never have let him go into danger without me at his back. No matter what he said. Let alone when there was such a clear threat."

"If you'd been there, the attacker might have got you."

"Then you could have given me your blood. We have to take care of each other."

"Agreed. But don't you think everyone is on alert now?"

"Of course. I just—"

"Think you can protect everyone better than anyone else?"

"Is that so shocking?"

"No. It's very much you."

"My family come first. But I have to protect them. I'm afraid I forgot that."

The garden gate clicked open. Raoul's wife Laura came into the garden, holding a piece of paper, the red seal broken. A gilded crest on the paper caught the sunlight. "We've received an invitation. From the Duke of Bamford—Tony—and Désirée. To Sawden Park. A thank you for our assistance. Désirée says she's a bit nervous hosting a house party and would appreciate our support. I must say it's difficult to imagine Désirée Clairineau being nervous about anything."

"She's never taken on the beau monde," Mélanie said. Memories of the early days of her marriage to Malcolm, and perhaps even more, when they had first settled in Britain, shot through her mind.

Raoul walked over to join them, Clara in his arms, the other three children trailing behind along with Berowne the cat.

"We're going to the country?" Colin asked, Berowne's lead in his hand.

"It looks like it," Mélanie said.

"I had a note from Tony yesterday saying they planned to invite us," Raoul said. "The duchess and John Wilcox will be there as well. And the Bamford children."

"Meaning Sylvie St. Ives," Mélanie said. Sylvie, the wife of Tony's heir, was an agent herself and a longtime opponent. She'd proved to be something of an ally in their latest adventure, but when it came to sources of danger Mélanie watched for, Sylvie was high on the list.

"Tony didn't say it outright, but I believe they plan to discuss plans for a divorce with the family," Raoul added.

"And they want us there?" Laura reached out to touch Clara's hair.

"Support can mean a lot," Raoul said.

"A sign of friendship," Malcolm said. "We should heed the call. We've certainly been grateful for the support of our friends through the years."

Jessica ran over to Mélanie and climbed into her lap. "I like Sophie."

"And I'm sure she'll be happy to see you," Mélanie said, wrapping her arms round her daughter.

"Are Tony and Désirée getting married?" Emily asked. Raoul and her mother had been a couple for over a year before Raoul had been able to get a divorce and they could marry, so she was well versed in the difference between marriage and commitment.

"It looks as though they'll be able to eventually," Raoul said. "Tony was afraid Désirée wouldn't agree to it, but from his letter it sounds as though he's got the nerve to ask and she's not averse to the idea."

"Why wouldn't she want to get married?" Jessica asked. At four and a half, she was fond of fairy tales and happy endings. And fortunately the marriages she'd observed close round her gave her no reason to doubt them. Including her own parents' marriage, which Mélanie had once worried would be a cause for concern.

"I don't think it's marriage," Raoul said. "It's marrying a duke. It rather goes against everything Désirée stands for. But she seems to be willing to come round."

"We all make compromises for love," Laura said.

Malcolm slid his arms round Mélanie and smoothed Jessica's hair. "So we do."

～

"A SOUJOURN IN THE COUNTRY." Julien Mallinson set down his coffee cup. "What could be more charming."

Kitty shot a look at her husband over Désirée Clairineau's letter of invitation, written on crested note paper. "Don't be difficult."

"On the contrary." Julien sat back in his chair, and folded his arms behind his head. "I have some very agreeable memories of country house parties. Always an excellent setting for a mission. If a bit challenging that one can't immediately leave."

Kitty set the invitation down beside her coffee cup. "Désirée and Tony are attempting to build a life together. The least we can do is be supportive."

"Oh, I quite agree. I admire anyone for doing the same. And having finally admitted to having friends, I'm all for supporting them. I think Bamford's deluding himself if he thinks inviting all his grown children to this house party will go smoothly, though."

Kitty took a sip of coffee. "You just don't want to see Sylvie."

"That too. Can you blame me?"

"Poor darling. Sylvie is unavoidable."

"Yes, but we'll be trapped in a house with her."

"You might be able to learn what she's planning."

Julien reached for his own coffee. "Sweetheart, did you just suggest I spend time with Sylvie?"

"I have no problem with your spending time with Sylvie. Except worries about what it may do to your sanity."

He grinned. "I'll survive. And you're right, we do need to know what she's planning. Aside from the fact that she's reporting to Castlereagh. I don't think the foreign secretary is the only one she's working for."

"Nor do I." Kitty glanced at the abandoned plates with toast crumbs, marmalade smears, and congealing egg that Leo, Timothy, and Genny had left. "The children will like the country. By the way, yesterday Timothy asked me how we met."

Julien frowned. "What did you say?"

"The truth. That we were on a mission."

Julien cast a glance through the open door across the passage to the library where the children were playing. "Did you say we were trying to work out if we were on the same side or enemies?"

"No, that seemed a bit much. One thing at a time."

"They're going to ask more questions."

"Long before we're ready to deal with them. Of course the thought of what they may work out on their own without asking questions is even more frightening."

Julien reached for the coffee pot and refilled their cups. "We can ask Tony and Désirée for advice. I'm sure Sophie's asked them similar questions. Or soon will."

CORDELIA DAVENPORT PAUSED in the doorway of the schoolroom where her husband Harry was drawing a timeline of first-century Roman history for their daughters Livia and Drusilla.

"That's wrong," Livia said. "Claudius became emperor in 41."

"Excellent," Harry said.

Livia regarded her father. "Did you really forget? Or were you trying to catch us?"

"Does it matter?" Harry said. "You're clever either way."

"Yes, but if you did it on purpose, I haven't caught you in an error."

Harry grinned. "I have no doubt you can be quicker than me, sweetheart. And will be on a great many occasions."

"Mummy!" Drusilla caught sight of Cordelia. Cleo, their dog, looked up and thunked her tail on Axminster carpet.

Cordelia smiled and moved into the room. "We've been invited to a house party. By the Duke of Bamford and Désirée Clairineau."

"Sophie!" Drusilla bounced on her chair.

"Yes. And the Rannochs and O'Roarkes and Julien and Kitty are invited too." Cordelia still couldn't call Julien and Kitty 'the Carfaxes' for all Julien had officially been Earl Carfax for over a year. "As well as the rest of the Bamford family."

"That should be interesting," Harry said.

Cordelia crossed to her husband's side. "Given our own lives, we should be particularly supportive when it comes to getting our friends through times like this." Though she and Harry had had to go through the worst times in their marriage separately.

"You mean a divorce?" Livia asked.

Cordelia bent to pet Cleo. "You listen all too closely, darling."

"I couldn't help but notice."

"I don't think it's the divorce that's the challenge so much," Harry said. "It's telling their children."

Livia wrinkled her nose. "You mean their children want them to be together even if they aren't happy?"

"Their children may have different standards for what makes a marriage."

Livia's straight brows drew together. "I didn't like it when you were apart. But I wouldn't like you to be unhappy. And Tony's children are grown up."

"Parents are still parents," Drusilla said.

Harry touched her fair hair. "Very true."

CHAPTER 4

June 1821
Sawden Park, Surrey

"*M*rs. Worthing was asking me about the room assignments." Désirée looked up from a sheet of paper she was scanning in the light from the salon's French windows. She felt too unsettled to sit. Much as she did in the planning stages of a mission.

Tony looked up from the writing desk in the corner of the salon. "Shouldn't be too complicated. I don't think there's anyone we need to strategically give rooms close together. Except Hetty and Wilcox."

"At least we're making more room by sharing a bedchamber. For that matter, I'm assuming most of the couples attending would prefer to share a bedchamber. Am I wrong?"

Tony got to his feet and moved to her side to scan the list. "I can't claim to have discussed sleeping arrangements with any of them, but I'm quite sure you're right. I know the Rannochs and O'Roarkes don't have separate rooms from when I visited after O'Roarke was wounded." He touched her hair.

"What?" Désirée looked up at him.

"I remember when we first stayed at the cottage in Normandy. Long before we thought we could have anything but a few weeks together. What was most remarkable was waking up with you. It seems such a simple thing now, but it was like nothing I'd ever imagined."

Désirée pressed her head against his shoulder, a gesture she once wouldn't have allowed herself. It took strength to let oneself show sentiment. "I won't argue with you there." She looked back at the list. The Rannochs and O'Roarkes and Carfaxes and Davenports were easy enough. But then there were Tony's children. "Rosalind wrote that Gaspar won't be able to accompany her. Helena and Toby may want to share a room. But I suspect St. Ives and Sylvie and Frederica and Percy will want separate rooms. And I think for now, Hetty and John will as well."

"Hetty might be fine with sharing a room, but I think it would be too much for Wilcox. John. And Hetty's probably worried about scandalizing the children. Odd how we go from the children scandalizing their parents to the parents scandalizing the children."

"I don't know that we'll ever be able to scandalize Sophie."

"There's something to be said for children growing up knowing their parents in full."

She looked down at the list again. "I can't believe I'm doing this."

"Planning sleeping arrangements?"

"Hosting a house party. I have a whole new appreciation for the challenges faced by political hostesses." Désirée scanned the list again. "You can't expect Sylvie and Rosalind at least not to play this for advantage."

His brows tightened. "It's a family situation."

"Tell me you've never played a family situation for every advantage you could."

Tony's frown deepened. "I don't quite see how they can use—"

23

"That doesn't mean they won't try."

"To do what?"

"I'm not sure. I don't understand the agenda of either of them. But I have to say I'm intrigued. In the case of your family, family life doesn't mean abandoning espionage at all."

"A point."

"It may help having the Rannochs here. And the O'Roarkes and Davenports and Carfaxes. They'll stay out of family drama but they can help with any espionage repercussions."

"That was my thinking. And I was thinking we could invite Franz as well. You should have family here too."

Désirée considered her nephew, presently lingering in London after their adventures the previous spring. "So he can be part of the chaos?"

"I was thinking that we're all family now, as you said."

"Ah."

"And I thought we'd invite Lisette Varon and her family. She and Franz could do with some time together."

Désirée smiled. "You're an incurable romantic, Tony."

"I never claimed otherwise."

"No, you've always been very honest about who you are." Désirée thought back to the last time she had seen her nephew in London before they left. So much had been unsaid, but she'd read how he was struggling with the next steps in his life. "It will be good for Franz to have some more time with Raoul and the Rannochs. He needs to sort out the sort of life he's going to have if he and Lisette are to have a future."

"I don't see anything in Franz's life that would prevent his having a future with Lisette."

"As an Austrian diplomat? In Metternich's service?"

"Lisette isn't known as a French agent."

"I'm not sure Lisette wants to go to Austria. She might be worried her past could cause problems for Franz. And she might not want to be the wife of one of Metternich's diplomats. It's all very well to be a romantic, Tony, but people have to find a way to make their lives work together."

"We did."

"By changing both our lives and hiding away from the world." Désirée glanced out the French windows. Sophie was playing with Belle in the artfully ruined folly that had once been the site of an unexpected adventure for her parents. "I didn't want to take you away from your work."

Tony laughed. "My darling. You spent more than two decades opposing my work as strenuously as possible."

"Not all of it. And that doesn't mean I don't want you to do what matters to you."

Tony glanced at their daughter, then looked back at her. "What matters to me is the one thing in my life that's made sense for the past two decades. You."

She choked. "That's quite lovely, Tony. But not enough—"

"You aren't an agent anymore." He grinned and brushed a curl back from her face. "At least not unless you're under very deep cover."

"I have my writing. And Sophie."

"Well, I have Sophie too. I'll work out the rest." He put his hands on her shoulders. "Don't think I regret leaving diplomacy for a moment. Franz isn't the only one questioning the government he serves."

Past quarrels and conversation—often in bed—echoed in her head. "Thank you."

"I don't think I'd be the man you love if I didn't do that."

"I don't think you'd be you, if you didn't do that."

"Took me long enough."

"You always questioned it, Tony. It's one of the reasons we worked together."

"One of the reasons you put up with me."

"One of the reasons I fell in love with you. Though I didn't admit it."

"Didn't admit the reason, or that you fell in love with me?"

"Both, perhaps." Désirée turned her mind back to her nephew Franz and his love, Lisette. "Lisette's sensible. I think she wants a life with Franz. But she's too sensible to change herself to make it work. Because she'd realize that wouldn't work at all."

A flicker of concern crossed Tony's face. "You didn't, did you?"

"Change myself? I've changed immeasurably. We all do. I may have changed because of you, in some ways. But I didn't change myself *for* you. We have what we have because we found a way to meet between our worlds."

Tony frowned. "I remember Mélanie Rannoch in Vienna. I didn't know a quarter of her story, but I sensed the brilliance. But I think she was changing herself to make her marriage work. Then and later. Don't tell Malcolm or O'Roarke. They'd be horrified."

"I suspect they know. And that they're horrified. I don't think she's doing that anymore, though. Though she's still playing the political wife."

Tony nodded. "I'd like time with O'Roarke myself. I'm a bit worried about him. That is, in some ways I'm less worried about him. I'm not as afraid he'll get himself killed. But I want to make sure he's all right with changing his life. Speaking of changing one's life."

"Yes, but he didn't do it because of Laura. Who strikes me as much too sensible to ask anything of the sort of him. He did it because of Malcolm. Changing one's life for one's children is rather different."

"And I also think he did it for himself."

"So do I. He wants time with his children. I can quite understand that. I knew I wasn't going into the field once Sophie was born. But I imagine he could use time to talk with a friend. He has a great deal to sort out."

"Don't we all," Tony said. "That is—"

"Quite right." Désirée touched his arm. "We're both still sorting things out. Though there was one thing I knew after Waterloo. We weren't enemies anymore. Something had shifted. And would shift permanently. I suppose that was when I first accepted I had a family."

Tony laughed with what sounded like wonder and relief. "Only you could put it that way, my darling." He leant in and kissed her. "One of the things I loved about you from the first was that you weren't afraid of risk. And perhaps this is the greatest of all."

"Becoming a duchess?"

"Risking one's feelings."

"It took me long enough to admit it. Though I knew a very long time ago. Long before I'd have admitted I believed in any such thing."

"What?"

She swallowed, but oddly the words didn't catch in her throat. "That you were the love of my life." She turned her gaze back to her list before she could make a complete fool of herself. "I know your grandchildren are used to staying in the nursery, but I think the Rannochs and O'Roarkes and Carfaxes and Davenports will want the children on the same floor—not in the nursery upstairs." The nursery Tony's older children had used. That they hadn't even considered for Sophie, who had a room next to theirs. "I'm thinking we can turn the Rose Room into a nursery—it's on a corner where it's close to all the parents."

"Excellent idea. You have a knack for this. I knew you would."

Désirée laughed. "You can't tell me you envisioned this when we met."

"Well, no." Tony grinned. "When we met, you had a knife to my throat."

CHAPTER 5

July 1797
Normandy

*H*is eyes were blue and fastened steadily on her face above the knife blade. "Go ahead. You quite have the advantage."

"I came here to kill you." She pressed the knife closer to his throat.

"Yes, I suspected as much." His gaze was unblinking in the moonlight. His head was on a drift of pine needles, one almost poking him in the eye, but he stayed motionless. "You're quite free to get on with it. I'm not in much of a position to stop you."

Désirée shifted her weight on her heels, keeping the knife steady. "That's rot. If you really thought you were going to be killed, there are all sorts of things you could do."

"You have a knife to my throat."

"If you thought you were going to be killed, it would be worth the risk."

"Fair enough. What would you do if our situations were reversed?"

"Knee you in the balls."

"Good thinking. I'll remember that if I live to see a future encounter."

"We're highly unlikely to encounter each other again," Désirée said. "Weren't you trying to kill me?"

"I was trying to take down an opponent. That was before I knew you were a—"

"Oh, god. Don't say it was before you knew I was a woman. I'm still an enemy agent."

"Permit me my quixotic impulses."

"It's old-fashioned enough to recall Don Quixote."

"If it's any comfort, I don't like killing in general."

"I don't like needless killing. Where are the papers?"

His gaze was focused, but lit with irony. "You can't imagine I'll just tell you."

"I'm holding the knife."

"And if you use it, I really won't be able to tell you."

An owl called in the tree branches overhead. She could hear the rushing of a stream just down the slope from them. She knew she had back-up, but there was no sign that he did. She sat back on her heels, the knife still at his throat. "Put your hands out."

He gave a faint smile and complied. She tugged a length of twine from her pocket with one hand, draped it over his hands, then quickly dropped the knife so she could tie both ends. As she was tying the knot, footsteps crunched on the underbrush. She looked up, all senses alert, then stilled at the familiar figure.

"Jacques. I told you I had this under control."

"Just checking." Jacques took two steps forwards, then stopped, taking in the scene. In one swift move, he lifted a pistol and leveled it straight at her.

She grabbed the knife and rolled to the side, down the hill. Her quarry rolled after her. A pistol shot whistled overhead.

Pain shot through her arm. They rolled further down the hill, breaking through prickly underbrush, and landed hard in stream water. Footsteps thudded. Her quarry grabbed a rock and took aim. Jacques thudded to the ground. Of one accord, she and her quarry stumbled through the stream in the opposite direction.

They both went still for a moment, listening. No sound of footsteps.

"Your colleague has turned," her quarry murmured.

"So it would seem."

"Any idea whom he's working for now?"

"You're the enemy."

"My dear. Surely you've learnt there are more than two sides."

"Fair enough. How did you get your hands free?"

"Caught the twine on a rock as we rolled down the bank." He tugged the remnants of twine from his wrists.

"Presence of mind."

"There are reasons I'm still alive." He gripped her arm and stared down at it in the moonlight. "He got you."

"Just a graze."

"Even grazes can fester." He pulled a flask from his pocket, and splashed brandy on her arm.

"You're well supplied."

"Comes in handy." He tugged off his cravat and bound it round her arm with deft precision, then held out a hand. "Can you walk?"

"It's my arm, not my legs." She accepted his hand, despite the impulse to clamber up the bank on her own. In truth the support was welcome.

A howl sounded in the distance. "Wolf," he said. "Not close enough to bother us."

Still holding her hand, he helped her up the stream bank, then paused to take his bearings. "This way."

"Where are we going?"

"I have a safe cottage nearby. We can dry off and I have supplies there to properly bandage you."

She regarded him for a moment, but she still had the knife,

now tucked into her shirt, and they needed somewhere to shelter. Besides, she didn't have the papers yet. Easier to get them in an enclosed space. She pulled the knife out. "All right. You're still my prisoner."

"Fair enough."

He led the way through pine and beech and oak, round moss-covered stones and fallen logs. No sign of habitation, no sound of a road, but they reached a clearing and the moonlight gleamed on the pale stone of a vine-covered building with a timbered roof and wooden shutters. Near the door, he reached under a rock while she watched carefully, the knife held at the ready, and straightened up holding a key. He unlocked the door and lead the way into a stone-floored passage. He unhooked a lamp from inside the door and pulled a flint from his pocket with slow, precise motions that wouldn't alarm her. The light revealed a passage with hooks for hanging clothing, a table and a bench. It gave onto a paneled room with gleaming furniture from the last century upholstered in tapestry, a Savonnerie rug that was soft underfoot, and a stone fireplace she could have practically walked into.

"This is your idea of a safe house?" she asked.

He set the lantern on the central table. "Doesn't it look safe?"

"It looks ostentatious."

"Who says you can't be comfortable while being safe?" He moved to a cabinet across the room. In the lamplight she could see that he had fair hair, adorned with leaves at present, and that his coat was plastered to his shoulders with stream water.

"Spoken like an aristocrat."

"How do you know I'm an aristocrat?"

She laughed. "Your voice."

"You wound me. I'm an agent. Surely you can master many voices."

"The way you move. And yes, that could also be put on. But it's your unshakeable assurance."

"I've been knocked down, had a knife held to me, been shot at, and fallen into the water. I'm not feeling very sure of anything." He jerked his head towards the cabinet. "There's a medical supply box in there. If you get it out, you won't have to worry it's actually a pistol and I'm going to shoot you."

She opened the cabinet—walnut, inlaid with silver gilt—and found a brass-bound box. One eye on him, she cracked the box open to see lint, scissors, a bottle of brandy. She carried the box carefully to the table and set it down. She kept hold of the knife. "You're still my prisoner." She was aware she was on rather shaky ground with that, but sometimes simply stating a position of power could be a tactical advantage.

"All right. But you won't be very good at keeping me prisoner if you give way to infection."

"More fool you, then, for trying to treat me."

"Possibly. Call it another quixotic impulse."

"Don Quixote would have made a terrible agent. You're far more skilled."

"Not saying a lot. Though I can usually tell windmills from dragons." He regarded her for a moment, then glanced round the room, and moved to pick up a blanket draped over the sofa back.

"What's that for?" she asked.

"I need to get at your arm. You can wrap this round yourself."

"Oh. I'm not a lady. I mean, I'm not missish. I'm not a prude."

"Perhaps I am. Indulge me."

She shrugged out of her damp coat, shifting the knife from one hand to the other (keeping hold of it was really an act of principle at this point; he could easily get a jump on her), then started on her waistcoat buttons and winced.

"Here." He undid the buttons with swift, gentle fingers, then unfastened her shirt cuffs with the same care.

"I don't think I can get it over my head," she said.

He nodded, moved behind her, and eased the shirt up carefully. Gently, but with nothing of the lover in his actions. It hurt.

Far more than she'd admit, but far less than if she'd tried to do it herself.

He set the shirt on the table beside her coat and waistcoat and draped the blanket over her good arm. She wrapped it round herself while he soaked lint with brandy, pulled off her makeshift bandage (which had begun to stick to her wound) and cleaned the wound. He was neat and methodical, but kept his attention meticulously focused on the wound. Gentlemanly reticence could be amusing. And useful. She almost laughed. Then she sucked in her breath as he eased a stubborn bit of cloth free of the wound.

"Sorry," he said. "You took a bit of the forest floor with you."

"It's all right." She'd felt worse. It really wasn't much more than a scratch, but rolling over dirt and leaves hadn't been good for it. He had a point. And infection would be awkward.

"Shouldn't take too long to heal. Do you think Jacques will send friends after you?"

"I'm not sure. I'm still trying to sort out whom he's working for."

He knotted off the ends of a clean bandage. "There's some better brandy on top of that cabinet. Do you trust me to pour?"

"I'm not quite sure how you'd hide a weapon in a decanter. Unless you're an enchanter."

"I fear my skills stop well short." He strolled to the cabinet, unstopped the decanter, and poured generous measures into two crystal glasses. "I hope this helps." He put a glass into her hand.

"You take chivalry too seriously," she said. "Or you're playing a very deep game."

"You're overthinking. Call it instinct."

"The instinct of chivalry?"

"The instinct of care for a fellow human." He touched his glass to hers.

She waited for him to drink first, just in case, then took a sip. It was a superb brandy, supple and fiery and much appreciated after the night's adventures.

He grinned and took another sip of his own. "You'll find some clean shirts in the second drawer of the cabinet."

She took another sip of brandy and retrieved a shirt. Fine linen. She dropped the blanket from her shoulders without embarrassment and pulled the shirt over her head. No harm in giving him a view of her back. She turned with a smile that was part challenge to find his gaze politely averted.

"I'm quite decent again."

He swallowed the last of his cognac. "If you'll trust me enough to follow me into the kitchen, it should be stocked with provisions. Nothing elaborate, but enough to make us a meal."

She hesitated just long enough to consider. But trust could be useful. And she didn't have a lot of other options. "I don't know whether to be more surprised that you have fresh provisions or that you know how to make a meal from them. Do lead the way."

CHAPTER 6

June 1821
Sawden Park, Surrey

"It looks charming. You've done an excellent job." Hetty set her hat down on the dressing table and smoothed the satin ribbons. "I hope that doesn't sound condescending."

"Not in the least," Désirée said. "I fully yield to your superior expertise. In fact, if you'd like to decide anything—it really is your house."

"My dear." Hetty regarded her across an expanse of Axminster carpet. "This house is emphatically yours and Tony's now. And legally will be when you marry."

"I'm not much for legalities, but by legalities it's still yours." Désirée cast a glance round the room, a pretty chamber hung with silk in an ice blue she'd observed was a favorite of Hetty's. Noting such things was helpful for an agent. "Do you like this room? I wasn't sure if you'd rather have—"

"My old room?" Hetty smiled.

"We aren't using it. That is—"

"You and Tony are sharing a chamber. Quite sensible even if

it's something I wouldn't have thought of. But having me just a dressing room away would be a bit odd."

"It's a very large dressing room. Though we've actually turned it into Sophie's room."

"An excellent use for it. But more to the point, we should set the tone now for how we mean to go on. Better to get everyone accustomed to our new roles. And rooms can be a powerful symbol. Besides, I've always liked this room. Rather better than the duchess's official chamber, I confess. But then I never spent a great deal of time here. This was always Tony's house. The place he'd go to be alone."

"I know, I—"

"Visited him?"

"I was delivering a warning."

"No need to apologize. I'm glad you had a taste of it. You need time to settle in. And from what I've seen, you are managing it beautifully."

"Spoken like a diplomat. This"—Désirée gestured round the room—"is hardly my area of expertise."

"I have no doubt you could master any skills you put your mind to acquire, Désirée. But there's no particular reason for you to do so in this case. At least, not for a decade or so."

"A decade?"

Hetty glanced towards the windows. The children—Sophie and Tony and Hetty's grandchildren—were outside playing on the lawn. "When you want to bring Sophie out."

For a moment cold horror closed Désirée's throat. "I hardly think Tony and I are ever going to move in the beau monde. Married or not, we'll always be a scandal."

"Oh, you'd be amazed at the wonders time can work in blurring lines of scandal." Hetty set her dressing case on the dressing table and snapped back the lid. "Look at Lady Cordelia. For that matter, look at the O'Roarkes. You're charming and the beau monde have a way of bending to accept eccentricities. Especially in those born at its heart. And Tony's a duke. That will always count for something. By the time Sophie's of marriageable age, you should be able to give her every advantage you wish." Hetty took out a pot of rouge and met Désirée's gaze. "Does that horrify you?"

"More than any mission I've undertaken."

"Yes, I can imagine that. I'll own those years I was chaperoning the girls were some of the most trying, though I also enjoyed the influence. At times I enjoyed the strategy. Well, a good deal, actually." She set a gilded crystal perfume bottle beside the rouge pot. "It was quite as challenging as the most complicated diplomatic negotiation I assisted Tony with. And just as tedious. If not more so. Not that the girls really let me orchestrate anything for them. They all were quite decided on what they wanted for themselves."

"Isn't that what we want for our children?"

"That's what Tony said. But you've met Percy. And Gaspar. And Sylvie, for that matter. Helena, I'll confess, managed it quite expertly. I'd never have chosen Toby for her. But then my own tastes were different, at least then. Now that I think about it, Toby is not unlike John."

"And perhaps a bit like Tony." Toby was the one of Tony's sons-in-law whom Désirée had got to know a bit.

"Yes." Hetty's brows drew together. "Perhaps a bit more like the man Tony is now. Or the way I see Tony now. In any case, after seasons of strategizing and maneuvering, the girls were all settled. And I realized there was no need to worry so much about how we positioned ourselves. How many balls and musicales we gave, and who attended. It's not that I don't enjoy entertaining, or that John and I don't intend to do so. But it will be rather a relief to do it on my own terms. The beau monde are decidedly more agreeable when no one is hunting for a husband." Hetty pulled a silver comb and brush from the dressing case. "I can't imagine your not doing anything on your own terms. But trust me, when Sophie is waltzing round a ballroom and you see her with a gentleman you don't think will make her happy, all your instincts about leaving her to her own choices will be severely strained."

Désirée folded her arms. "That's assuming I want her to marry at all. I never wanted to do so."

"And yet now you are."

"So I am. And I hope Sophie is as happy as I am. But I wouldn't assume the path to that happiness lies in a certain way. Yet if it did seem to lie through a London season"—a host of images, most of them uncomfortable, shot through Désirée's mind—"I'd do my best to make it happen. Just because I may disapprove of something doesn't mean she should live her life according to my principles."

Hetty's mouth curved in a smile. "It isn't easy."

"Navigating the beau monde?"

"Being a parent."

SILENCE GRIPPED THE SALON. None of Tony and Hetty's children seemed to be able to find the words to answer the announcement their parents had just made. It was the sort of scene Désirée would have once found amusing. If she hadn't been in the middle of it. If it hadn't involved the man she loved and the family that were now, one way or another, her own. She was sitting to the side, as was John Wilcox. She cast a quick glance at him and met his pained gaze. He would rather be anywhere but here. His being here for Hetty spoke volumes about his feelings for her.

Rosalind, Tony and Hetty's youngest child, found her voice first, blue eyes wide with indignation. "You can't."

Hetty regarded her youngest daughter. "That's not normally something children say to their parents."

"But why on earth do you want to?" Rosalind asked. "It's not as though anyone's asking you to give up—anything. Everyone has—"

"Not everyone," Helena, their second daughter, said. She was sitting quietly on the settee beside her husband Toby Ludgrove, their arms brushing. Toby had reached out in the midst of the announcement and gripped his wife's hand.

"You know what I mean." Rosalind rounded on her sister, then turned back to their parents. "You can have your amusements without creating a scandal."

"Have to say Rosy has a point." St. Ives, the heir to the dukedom, scraped the toe of his boot over the polished salon floor. "That is"—he coughed—"no intention to offend anyone. But surely there's no need to tarnish the family with divorce."

"Our family have weathered an attainder, two annulments, five charges of treason, and at least ten duels," Tony said. "I think the Southcott name can weather your mother and I civilly deciding to end our marriage."

Rosalind turned back to Helena. "Say something. You're supposed to believe in happy marriage."

"I do. Which is why I don't think two people should be asked to stay in one if they aren't happy." Helena tightened her grip on her husband's hand and smiled at her parents. "I'm glad you've both found people to make you happy."

"Oh, for god's sake." St. Ives looked at his eldest sister. "Say something, Freddie."

"What is there to say?" Frederica asked. She was sitting on a straight-backed chair, across the room from her husband Percy Rawdon. "It sounds as though Mama and Papa have found a very sensible way to manage things. I can only applaud their good sense."

St. Ives threw up his hands and took a turn about the hearth rug.

"Do stop prowling about, St. Ives," Hetty said. "This needn't concern you."

"What do you mean?" St. Ives turned to his mother. "Of course it concerns us."

"I have to say your mother's right," Sylvie St. Ives said. "It's their choice and we clearly aren't going to talk them out of it."

Rosalind spun towards her brother's wife. "That woman is going to be Duchess of Bamford."

"That woman," Tony said, in a voice of carved ice, "is the mother of your sister and is the woman I love. Say what you will to me, but leave Désirée out of it."

"We can't," Rosalind said. "You've put her in the middle of it."

Tony's gaze swept his children. In that moment, Désirée wanted to hug him as though he were Sophie when she'd taken a tumble or a game had turned out badly. But no such simple comfort would work. One could say he had bungled this badly, but really, no other approach had been possible. "Your mother and I," Tony said, with the level gaze she'd seen him give to junior agents, "have made a choice that's best for our futures. We won't let it impact any of you."

"That's rot." St. Ives's head snapped in his father's direction. "It can't help but impact us."

Tony met his son's gaze. "Only if you choose to let it."

Hetty smoothed her hands over her sprigged muslin skirt. A country dress, but still the dress of a duchess. "You might consider that neither your father nor I are asking your permission or your blessing or even your opinions. Any more than we expect you to ask the same of us at this point in your lives."

Rosalind stared at her mother. "You're going to marry a steward."

"Apologize to your mother," Tony said. "That was uncalled for."

"Why? It's nothing but the truth. Wilcox won't deny it, I'm sure."

"John Wilcox is one of the best men I know." Tony nodded at Wilcox, who was still sitting by in silence. "Your mother loves him. We should all be pleased to see those we love find happiness."

"Some of us wouldn't know about that," Sylvie said. "Sorry."

Rosalind shook her head, her blonde ringlets stirring round

her face. "It turns everything on its head. Everything you ever told us."

"I'm sorry." Hetty's gaze settled on her daughter. "Truly."

"Don't be. At least you raised us with the right principles. Now you're throwing them away."

"Then you'll have to put it down to eccentricity," Tony said. "There's been plenty of that in the Bamford family through the years. Your mother and I won't embarrass you. We both mean to live quietly. You can get on with your lives and shake your heads at our foolery if you wish. It needn't concern you."

"But it does," Rosalind said. "That's what being a family means. Unless you mean to say we were never family at all."

CHAPTER 7

July 1797
Normandy

*D*ésirée's erstwhile quarry lifted the lamp and led the way to a cool, tiled kitchen with a deal table and a cooler from which he produced hard cheese, bread, eggs, and an array of vegetables.

"Who on earth stocks this?" she asked. "You have people bring food just in case you happen to be here?"

"Doesn't that make sense? You have to admit it's useful tonight." He struck a spark to the coals in the range, unhooked a pan from the wall, and cracked five eggs. A few minutes later they had omelettes, warm bread, and cheese.

She watched him from her seat across the table as he slid a plate towards her. He opened another cabinet and studied an array of wine bottles. "This vintage was good the last time I had it," he said, setting one on the table. He extracted the cork, took two glasses from a shelf, filled them, and passed one to her.

She took a sip. Rich and earthy, but supple and smooth. "I

suppose I shouldn't be surprised. I've heard about officers who take crystal glasses and crates of port into battle."

"I've never gone into battle. But I can imagine the impulse. Though unless I brought enough for the company, I can't quite imagine facing the others."

"That rather gets to what we're fighting about."

"Wine?"

"Sharing."

"Ah. A good way of putting it." He sat back in his chair. "I have nothing against sharing."

"No. Some aristos are generous with their bounty. On their own terms. When they feel like it. It doesn't change the inequity."

He took a drink. "I don't deny the inequity."

She took a bite of the omelette. It was surprisingly well cooked. The vegetables were savory yet crisp, and the cheese was as superb as the wine. "Yet you support the Royalists."

"I support my country."

"Who support the Royalists."

"Do you support everything your country does?"

She choked on a bite of toast. "Hardly."

"Well, then."

"But I don't support my country simply because it's my country. I believe in change."

"I wouldn't say I don't believe in what Britain stands for."

"Which is?"

"Stability, for want of a better word."

"Which is excellent for those in power retaining their power."

"And yet it's often the most vulnerable who are crushed when things are overturned."

"I can't entirely argue with that. But you can't tell me you believe the argument that the least bit of change is one step away from revolution."

"No." He spooned some more omelette onto her plate. "But I thought you believed in revolution."

"I do. It's all very well to take change slowly, and I agree it can be risky, but it tends to be less risky for those in power in the first place."

"You have a powerful speaking style. Pity France hasn't changed enough to allow women in the Assembly."

"Yes, it is. So I have to find other ways to fight." She leant back in her chair, then winced at the pull on her wound.

He moved quickly, lunging out of his chair. "Are you—"

"I'll be all right." She smiled at him. "You're quite a mother hen."

"I have three children."

"And a devoted wife?"

"My wife is a brilliant woman with her own interests."

"Somehow I don't think they tend to stealing documents."

"No, though I imagine she'd be quite good at strategizing missions if she put her mind to it. She's brilliant at strategizing a London drawing room. Which can contain far more daggers than the average mission."

"Thank god there are some situations I'm spared."

"I'm sure you'd be quite good at it."

"But I can't imagine anything more hideous. Some challenges can also seem hopelessly stifling." She took another bite of omelette. "But then you must agree, to a degree."

He sat back in his chair. "What makes you think that?"

"The English ton is your world. But you're here."

"Ah." He twisted his glass between his fingers. The candlelight bounced on the rich red. "Some would say I never got over being a schoolboy who wanted to run away and fight dragons. Save that I always wanted to tame them and fly with them."

"That's the most interesting thing you've said all night."

"There are limits. To how much one can escape. But I'll own I feel the most myself—here. Meaning—"

"On a mission?"

He took a drink of wine. "Yes." He stared into the glass. "Or rather—in a world where position doesn't matter."

She took another drink of the wine, savoring its supple bite. "And yet you live surrounded by the trappings of your position."

"Caught."

"Mind you, I'd be even more shocked if you left it all behind and slept on the hard ground."

"I've been known to do that. But I see no reason to do so when circumstances don't require it." He refilled their wine. "Did you come here with Jacques?"

Her fingers stilled on the stem of her glass.

"You needn't answer. But if you're trapped here without a horse or carriage or any way to get to safety, you're too sensible not to tell me. There's a limit to how far even you are going to get on foot. Especially with an injured arm."

"Damn it." She snatched up her glass and took a drink. "I hate it when someone scores a point."

"I'm sure it doesn't happen often."

"You'd be surprised."

"I have horses nearby. I can get you to Paris. Or wherever you want to go."

"Have you forgot you're my prisoner?" She didn't try to disguise the irony as she said it.

"You can tie me up and pull me along with you if you choose."

"I'm not really in a position to tie you up. Not unless you let me do it to humor me. Which would be worse."

He flung back his head and laughed. "You don't strike me as someone who needs humoring."

"I'm sure you have excellent papers. But Paris isn't the safest place for you to be running about."

"I didn't become an agent to be safe."

"Meaning you have someone to meet there."

"Take it as you will. But you can always use it as an excuse to spy on me."

"I'm still the enemy, you know. Drinking wine and eating your excellent omelette doesn't change that."

"I'd never presume to think so. But you do need rest. I can keep watch while you sleep. I promise you needn't worry about interference—of any sort."

"You're the sort who takes being a gentleman seriously. Though I wouldn't put it past you to search my pockets. You're obviously not an incompetent agent."

"Thank you. From you I think that's a compliment."

"It is." She pushed back her chair. "It seems I don't have a great deal of choice but to trust you. It's a chill night." She got to her feet, as though to warm her hands at the stove. Easy enough to knock the iron door open with her knee while in the same instant she reached in her pocket and tossed the papers on the fire. The list of agents went up in flames. Which was fine, because the point of her mission had been to take back the list he had stolen and keep it from falling into British hands.

She heard his chair scrape back and turned to meet his gaze.

"My compliments," he said. "When did you take them?"

"When you were bandaging my wound. You were at such pains to be chivalrous you were distracted. And I still had one hand free."

"Clever. To burn them."

"No risk of your stealing them back. And my goal was to keep them out of your hands."

"Mission accomplished. May I now show you to your bedchamber?"

"You're still offering to get me to Paris?"

"My dear. After this evening, haven't you learnt I'm a gentleman? I can't not see a lady home."

CHAPTER 8

June 1821
Sawden Park, Surrey

"The night we met, you told me you were happiest on a mission. Away from"— Désirée gestured round the damask-hung bedchamber—"all this."

Tony shrugged on his blue superfine coat. "So I did."

"And yet we're living here."

He slid his arm round her. "I don't think I ever said I disliked England. I said I disliked living in the trappings of my position."

"What do you call our surroundings?"

"Extraordinarily pleasant. But at present, while we might be said to be enjoying the trappings of my position, I'm not being weighed down by it. Perhaps it's unfair to be enjoying the one without putting up with the other." He put his lips to her hair. "Are you saying you want to go somewhere else?"

"No. Much as I resisted the idea of England, I admit we have more freedom here at present than we would other places. It's better for Sophie. And you love it."

He lifted his head. "Don't be absurd."

"I'm not." She stood back in the circle of his arm and looked up at him. "You love your country. In a rather romantic, improbable way, but I understand. You're improbably romantic about a number of things. I love my own country. But I can't bear to be there now. And I think this is the best place for us to be as a family."

His gaze shifted over her face. "Once again, who are you and what did you do with Désirée?"

"We are a family. We agreed to be one after Waterloo. I never had a family before, so you can't blame me for sounding different about it."

He smoothed her hair back from her face.

She leant against his shoulder. "Besides, I admit it's a comfortable house. And you always did like your creature comforts. So did I. Rather more than I admitted that first night."

"Yes, well, there's a lot we didn't admit that first night."

"So there is." She lifted her head. "We have a house full of guests about to arrive. We need to go down."

"Pity. There are so many more interesting things we could do."

Désirée smiled and stepped back. "It was your idea to have a house party. And never let it be said I didn't strategize a mission well."

"Has this become a mission?"

"Oh, dearest." Désirée moved to the door. "Surely you know it's been a mission from the first."

COLIN, Jessica, Emily, and Clara tumbled from the carriage, seconds after the Davenport girls and seconds before Julien and Kitty's children. Not surprising, as they'd all driven in convoy from Mayfair so they could stop at the same inns. Mélanie took Malcolm's hand and climbed from the carriage, holding the basket their cat Berowne was in.

Sophie let go her mother's hand and ran forwards to greet them with none of the shyness she'd shown when they'd first met, her brown-and-white running after her.

"I like your house," Jessica said, bending to pet the puppy. Livia and Drusilla Davenport ran after her, their own dog Cleo following.

"There's a staircase with a railing you can slide down. And a castle. Over there." Sophie gestured towards a folly created to look like a medieval ruin. "My cousins are there."

A number of other children, ranging from teenagers to toddlers, were clustered round the folly. Tony's grandchildren, presumably. Technically Sophie's nieces and nephews, though cousins did make more sense.

"Wizard!" Timothy Ashton, Kitty's second son, stared at the folly. "Can we go see it?"

Sophie glanced at her parents, who nodded, and the children ran off towards the folly, Emily carrying Clara, and Leo Ashford carrying his little sister Genny. The two dogs raced after, already becoming fast friends.

Désirée smiled. "It's good for her to have children to play with. And good to see her seeing this as home. Thank for you coming."

"Thank you for having us," Mélanie said. "It's beautiful."

"Always a favorite place," Tony said. "Though far better with Désirée and Sophie."

"It's the people who make a home," Julien said. "Speaking as one who never thought of having a home until I had a family. Which I never thought of having either."

Sawden Park had the bones of an Elizabethan manor, considerably embellished in the last century. Wings stretched out to either side. Not as much of a castle as Dunmykel, Malcolm's Scottish house, but Mélanie could imagine how it felt to Désirée to suddenly be mistress of such a house.

Tony and Désirée led them into an entrance hall paneled in dark wood but with a raised ceiling and painted cupola and with a passage leading to an airy salon with French windows opening onto a terrace.

"It's always felt like a family house," Tony said.

Which it did. Just a very lavish one.

Hetty, still the Duchess of Bamford, at least for the moment, was seated in the salon, along with a tall, thin man with graying sandy hair who must be John Wilcox, and her eldest daughter Frederica Rawdon, tall and fair-haired like Hetty. And Frederica's husband Percy, who was slouched in a corner with a glass of brandy.

"How lovely." The duchess got to her feet. "We saw the children running across the lawn with Sophie. I don't believe any of you has met John Wilcox?"

Wilcox exchanged civil, polite greetings, though he looked a bit like a man who wasn't sure of the terrain he's stumbled into. Frederica got to her feet to hug Cordy, who was a friend, and greet the others. Percy nodded from his corner.

They settled themselves on sofa and settees. Mélanie took Berowne from his basket and held him against her shoulder. He purred and then swiveled his head towards the door, seconds before it opened to admit St. Ives and Sylvie.

"Don't stand on ceremony," Tony said. "You know everyone."

"Nothing like old friends," Sylvie said, with a smile that embraced the crowd and lingered on Julien.

St. Ives inclined his head to the company with a clenched jaw and the air of one determined to shoulder through.

Helena, the Bamfords' second daughter, came into the room next, through the French windows from the terrace, accompanied by her husband Toby Ludgrove. She had smooth blonde hair like her sisters and her mother's warm smile, with less of the duchess's formality. "I'm so glad you're all here. We were out by the folly with the children. They're thrilled to have so many other children to play with. And my little sister is clearly entranced."

"Rosy's by the folly?" St. Ives asked.

"Sophie."

"Oh." St. Ives coughed.

"Tea, I think," the duchess said. "That is—" She looked at Désirée.

"An excellent idea," Désirée said. "I'll speak to Thomas."

The door opened again and Rosalind burst into the room. "Well. I can't remember the last time we were all gathered together like this. Though I suppose we have too many guests to call it a family party." She cast a bright smile round the room. "But I'm sure it will be quite delightful. Nothing like time to relax with friends."

CHAPTER 9

*M*élanie stepped through the French windows and cast a quick glance round the terrace and the lawn beyond. The shadows of late afternoon slanted over the scene. A mock battle was in progress in the folly. Leo Ashford, Livia, and Emily were defending it from an onslaught by Colin, Sophie, Jessica, Drusilla, and Timothy Ashford, with an assortment of the Southcott grandchildren on either side and the dogs running cheerfully back and forth. Clara and Genny had another game in progress with Rosalind's daughters. Peaceful. Serene. The English countryside. But she'd learnt what dangers could lurk in serenity.

Raoul had been helping the children fashion sticks into swords, but he was moving back towards the terrace. "It's the Norman conquest, apparently," he told her, climbing the steps to the terrace. "A singularly apt choice given the allegiances of many of their parents."

He lurched to the side as he climbed the last step. Mélanie moved quickly to catch his arm. His legs still gave out at odd times and they'd all got used to watching for it.

Raoul smiled down at her as she gripped his arm. "I'm not

going to collapse, *querida*. And it's even less likely an assassin will burst through the shrubbery."

Mélanie drew her hand back. Though not until after he was on the terrace and she'd felt he was steady on his feet. "Is it that obvious?"

"Well, I do know you rather well."

"You can't blame me." Those moments in Berkeley Square, watching him lie pale against the sheets, and then later, waiting in the library during the transfusion, haunted her memory. Cold terror, such as she had rarely known it. The possibility of losing someone who had been integral to her life since before she turned sixteen. "It shook all of us. Nothing's the same."

"No. But it wasn't your fault."

"Of course it wasn't."

"But?" His eyes were sharp and steady.

Mélanie forced herself to meet his gaze. The gaze of her former spymaster. Her former lover. But more important, the gaze of her friend. "I watched you go out that door in the Tavistock, Raoul. I knew you'd been shot at an hour before. I knew the same people who'd tried to kill Tony Bamford were after you. And I just sat there and assumed—I'm not sure what I assumed. But I stayed there being a playwright and a mother and Malcolm's wife, and yes, a political hostess, and I assumed you'd be all right."

"As I have been a score of times. I am rather skilled at looking after myself."

"Tell me you'd have let me—or any of us—go off alone in the same circumstances."

"It's not quite the same thing."

"No." Her fingers bit into her arms below the puffed muslin sleeves of her gown. Pintucked, flounced, sashed in rose. The gown of a country lady. "Because I've changed. Because I've let myself change."

"Of course you have. You're not an agent anymore."

"I'm a playwright. Which I want to be. I'm a mother. Which, god knows, I want to be." She cast a quick smile at the children. Emily leaning out of the folly to tilt against Jessica. "But I can't let go of being an agent. I don't want to start thinking like a—"

"Civilian?"

"Like a beau monde wife." The words were torn from her. "I swore I wouldn't ever be one, and I let it happen without realizing it. I'm the one who knows situations like that. Like the one you walked into when you left the Tavistock. Better than Malcolm. Better than any of us but Julien. I can't let go of that side of myself. I didn't want to. Or if I did, I've realized how wrong I was."

He touched her arm with light fingers. "I'm all right."

"Barely." His gaunt face. Malcolm's pale face. Laura's eyes filled with horror. Julien's gaze wide with a terror she'd never seen. "We were lucky. I'm not going to let it happen again."

"It's not likely to happen again. Especially now I'm not in the field. I did that for all of us."

"And I couldn't be more grateful. To you and to Malcolm for asking you. But it doesn't make the risk go away. And I'm not going to stand by again."

"It's not your responsibility, *querida*."

"Oh, yes, it is. I'm responsible for my family. Before anything." She touched his arm. Reassuringly solid. Yet anything one could touch could be torn away in an instant. "And you're part of my family. In the end, after everything, that's what we are."

RAOUL TURNED as Tony came out of the salon onto the terrace. Malcolm had come out a few minutes before, and he and Mélanie had gone to join the children by the folly, where the Norman conquest was still in progress.

Tony paused beside Raoul, taking in the scene across the lawn. "Amazing how they can be happy in the moment. I always loved that with my older children, though I'm not sure I paused enough to appreciate it properly."

"It's different, being a parent at this age." Raoul regarded his friend. "You look happy."

"I am. It's what we had in Normandy. Only no goodbyes hanging over us. I was afraid Désirée would be restless. But so far, she seems happy. We'll have to see where life takes us."

"That's always the case."

Tony slanted a look at him. "Are you happy with where it's taken you?"

The constant question that lurked in the gaze of his family and friends, though none of them, even his wife, could quite put it into words. "Raimundo came to London. I've given him information about my networks. I may go to Spain occasionally. But nothing like before."

"And for yourself?"

Raoul drew a breath of the fragrant air, tinged with the cool of approaching evening. "I'm thinking of standing for Parliament. Does that make you laugh?"

"By no means. Parliament would be the better for you."

"You don't mean that."

"My politics are more aligned with yours than you realize. Even more aligned than they once were. But there's a need for a range of ideas articulately expressed. Yours need a voice."

"So people can listen politely and vote the other way?"

Tony glanced at Malcolm, bending to help Clara pick daisies. "Surely you don't think that's all your son is doing?"

"I think Malcolm fears it is, sometimes. But no. I don't. Nor Julien in the Lords. Nor David Mallinson or Roger Smythe or a score of others I could name. It's a different life. But one I could imagine. I feel rather as though I'm learning to walk."

"You were badly wounded."

"But that isn't why." Raoul watched Emily tilt with Sophie with wooden swords.

Tony followed his gaze. "I went to Normandy as much as I could, the past six years. Weeks, even months at a time. But I still missed too much. I'm not sure what else I need to be doing. Or want to do. But I know what my first priority is. And yet I hate myself sometimes." He looked out across the mist-dampened lawn at the Norman conquest reenactment.

"My dear fellow," Raoul said. "Why?"

"Any number of reasons. But when I remember how I first met Désirée. My marriage had long since changed into—what it is now, I suppose. Or close to it. Désirée fascinated me from the first. I knew we had no future, but I also knew what was between us wasn't idle. Yet at the same time, it never occurred to me that she was in the same category as a woman I'd marry."

Memories clogged Raoul's brain. "You were already married."

"Yes, but even then—it didn't occur to me to regret that I couldn't marry her, because it didn't occur to me for years that I ever might have married her. There were the girls one courted. And there were other women." Tony's fingers closed on the stone balustrade. "What an appalling way to frame it. How unfair to her. How unfair to Hetty."

"It's hardly unusual to see it that way."

"No." Tony shot a look at him. "But I don't think you ever did."

"No. But my background was a bit different."

"I'd like to think I could see beyond my background."

"Which you have."

Tony's gaze moved back to the lawn. Colin was sweeping a bow to Sophie, who appeared to be being crowned queen. "I look at Sophie and can't bear the thought of a man ever seeing her that way—"

Raoul remembered the first time he'd looked down at Emily asleep, as he carried her from a carriage into an inn parlor. Long before he'd had anything but a vague hope of a future with Laura. "There's nothing like having daughters to bring it home."

"I should have seen it with my older daughters. But we were all too much a part of the same world. And they seemed happy with their roles in it." Tony shook his head. "Folly to refine upon the past as I keep saying. All we can do is try to move forward more coherently."

Raoul leant against the balustrade and turned to look at Tony. "Désirée's changed as well."

Tony raised a brow.

"She's willing to marry you. She wouldn't have been."

Tony flung back his head and gave a shout of laughter. "A good point. Neither of us thought in terms of marriage twenty years ago, for different reasons. A lot's possible now that wouldn't have been twenty years ago."

"I think Hetty would agree."

"Oh, I'm sure she would." Tony's gaze narrowed. "All these years married. And I think Hetty and I've talked more honestly the past few weeks than ever before." He looked down at his fingers on the stone. "I'd have said I loved Hetty when we married. I did love her. But it wasn't—it wasn't like what I found with Désirée. Everything changed once I met her." Tony looked out across the lawn towards the birch trees. "There wasn't anyone else. Not that I'd ever been particularly active in that way. Oh, there was, a bit. After Hetty and I began to drift apart. We both started exploring. But once I met Désirée—I knew before I admitted it to myself. Years—decades—before I dared admit it to her." He gripped the edge of the balustrade. "That I was set for life and there was no turning back."

"A nerve-wracking realization, perhaps," Raoul said. "But there's also something reassuring in knowing that."

"So there is. It's perhaps why nothing else in my life has quite made sense these past years. And why I feel more at home now than I ever have. But I can't say at all the same for Désirée."

"I think she's at home with you and Sophie."

Tony smiled as Sophie knighted Colin with one of the stick swords Raoul had helped fashion. "Yes, I think she is. But this isn't a place she'd have chosen as home or a world she'd have chosen to live in."

"She's extraordinarily adaptable." Raoul looked at the children again. "And knowing Désirée, I wouldn't be surprised if she conquers Britain as your daughter just did."

CHAPTER 10

*M*élanie looked up from gathering up the stick swords that had been surrendered when the battle in the folly came to an end and glanced towards the terrace. Raoul and Tony were leaning against the balustrade.

Malcolm took the stick swords from her hand and added them to the pile he'd collected. "Do you think he's happy?" he asked.

"Tony Bamford? I think he's ridiculously happy, for all the challenges of his life now."

"Raoul."

Mélanie looked up at her husband in the lengthening shadows. "He wouldn't be human if he didn't have twinges of regret, darling. But you can see the strain that's lifted." She watched Raoul dig his shoulder into one of the pillars. "He's not being pulled in different directions. He seems at peace with it."

"At peace isn't happy. I don't want him to lose—"

"What?"

Malcolm's gaze moved over the line of birch trees in the distance. "The fire, I suppose. He's been so driven as long as I can remember."

"And you told me as long as you could remember you've worried if he'd survive to see you again."

"That's true."

Mélanie waved to Jessica, who had run out of the folly to set a daisy crown on Clara's head. "Forget worrying you wouldn't see him again for a moment. A child shouldn't have to say goodbye to a parent so often. Emily and Clara shouldn't have to."

"Are you trying to make me feel better, or yourself?"

"Both of us, perhaps. But I also think it's true." She waved to Colin, who was watching them. He didn't miss a lot. "Or perhaps I just need to believe it is."

Malcolm tucked the sticks under one arm and waved to Laura, who was coming from the steps from the terrace. He reached for Mélanie's hand. "Let's get some time with the children."

"Good idea. We'll need to change for dinner before long."

Malcolm grimaced. "I think we may be in for fireworks, but not the sort you were worrying about in Berkeley Square. And I'm not sure we can protect Tony and Désirée except by giving them cover and perhaps sympathies. We're in the midst of a domestic drama, not an international intrigue."

"In our family—not to mention the Bamford family—the two are frequently intertwined."

"Right now, I think what they need is cover."

Mélanie let him draw her towards the folly, where a mock coronation banquet was in progress. He was right. In a way. But she wasn't going to let her instincts down. She cast a last glance over her shoulder. Artful topiary, beds of lavender, a tumbling fountain, roses that looked wild but were no doubt carefully cultivated. The garden looked tranquil. And experience taught that the most tranquil settings could be the deadliest.

60

DÉSIRÉE LEANT against the balustrade beside Raoul. Tony had gone to join Mélanie and Malcolm and Laura O'Roarke, who were playing with the children. "Tony seems to have been pressed into service knighting the victors in the recent battle."

"So it appears. A good role for a duke, don't you think?"

"Far less troublesome than some things dukes could get up to." She grinned. "When we met, I'd never have thought to find either of us in this position."

"A year ago, I'd never have thought to find either of us in this position," Raoul said. He was leaning easily against one of the pillars of the terrace, but he still didn't move with quite the lithe ease he'd had before he'd been wounded.

She smiled. "You look happy. But I know you enough to know it must be hard. I couldn't entirely avoid regrets, at moments, in Normandy."

"And yet you made the decision before I did."

She didn't pretend not to understand what "the decision" was. Though it hadn't seemed like such a decision after Waterloo. More inevitable. "I was the only one to take care of Sophie. And part of it was purely for myself—I didn't want to miss watching her grow up. And didn't think I could trust anyone else with her."

"I never wanted to miss any of it either. I missed too much with Malcolm. But I've also missed too much with Emily and Clara. I should have made the decision sooner."

"The world is harder on women."

He gave a crooked smile. "You're rather kindly not calling me a selfish idiot."

"We all make choices. We all have to define our priories. Mine shifted."

"And mine didn't soon enough."

She folded her arms and tilted her head to the side. "I remember you talking about Malcolm from the beginning. Even that first night Tony and I picked you up at the coast, when you fled Ireland. You were careful not to say too much. But it was clear how much you missed him. How proud of him you were. How much you loved him. I was nineteen and thought how fortunate I was not to have ties that could interfere with my work. It was a long time before I could admit that I might be missing those ties. By Vienna, I envied you."

"By Vienna, I'd compromised my relationship with my son to the extent I'd broken it."

Désirée glanced at the lawn in front of the folly, where a court ball now seemed to be taking place. Malcolm was dancing with Emily. "Palpably untrue."

"I've been fortunate. Which is one reason I owe Malcolm this."

"But don't do it just because you owe him."

"I'm not. I made the decision for myself. All choices have consequences. I'm still discovering the consequences of this one." He watched her for a moment. "Talking of which, you've made some rather consequential choices yourself. Normandy was one thing."

"And the English countryside is different?"

"The fact that it's England, perhaps. But I was thinking more that it's—"

"Not a cottage?" Désirée glanced over her shoulder at the windows opening onto a vista of mirrors reflecting the gleaming walls hung with figured silk damask, the paintings bought up on generations of grand tours, the gilded en-suite furniture. "It's certainly not anywhere I expected my life to take me. I can't imagine doing it if Tony wanted to continue his old life. That is, I suppose I'd have to work out something, as I quite want to be with Tony. But it's difficult to imagine being the sort of duchess Hetty was. But for the moment I think I can make this work. We'll see what happens if Tony decides he wants something else."

Raoul dug his shoulder into the pillar. "Tony's not going to want anything but you. He hasn't for a long time."

"But one's life never comes down to a romantic partner, does it? I'd never let that be said about a woman, so I really can't say it about a man. I suppose the difference is Tony and I both have to take the other one into account now when we work out what we want. That's distinctly odd. I used to think it made any permanent relationship impossible. But now I confess I can see the compensations."

Raoul's gaze went to his wife, who had her arms round their elder daughter and Jessica Rannoch. "I haven't made enough decisions taking Laura into account. And she's been very careful never to ask me to."

"Wise woman. It's one thing to change to be with one's partner. It's quite another to have one's partner ask one to change. I'd never have forgiven Tony if he'd asked me. And I'd never have asked him."

CHAPTER 11

June 1816
Normandy

ésirée peered through the window. The features of the person walking down the path weren't clear yet, but she'd know that compact, loose-limbed gait anywhere. She went out the door of the cottage, Sophie at her hip, and walked down the path to meet him. Odd how the first night she'd come here, in the dark, she hadn't even realized there was a path. The wind tugged at her hair and brought the scent of lavender. Sophie looked round with wide eyes. Désirée would swear her daughter was as excited as she was herself.

He stepped between two trees, and there he was. In trousers and a plain cloth coat, but he'd always unmistakably be a duke, unless he was on a mission. He dropped the bag he was carrying, leant in to kiss her, and pressed a kiss to Sophie's head. Sophie stretched out a hand. Tony took her from Désirée's arms and swung her round. Sophie giggled in delight.

"She's missed you," Désirée said.

Tony grinned and held Sophie against his shoulder. "I was afraid she wouldn't remember."

"She has quite a good memory."

He shot a look at her.

"I can tell. She reacts to things and people she hasn't seen for weeks. I may be not experienced with babies, but who's better at observing than a spy?"

Tony grinned. "A good point." He smiled down at Sophie as she stretched up a hand to the day's growth of beard on his cheek. "The truth is I don't think I spent as much time with my other children when they were babies as I have with her, for all I was in the same house much of the time." He smiled at Désirée over their daughter's head. "You aren't the only one whose priorities have changed."

Désirée watched him settle Sophie against his shoulder. He had an easy comfort with babies for all he said he'd spent less time with his older children. He'd been easier holding Sophie than she had at first. She remembered the first moment the doctor had put Sophie in her arms, and Tony leaning over to encircle both of them.

"I saw Franz," Tony said, as they walked into the cottage, Tony holding Sophie in one arm and his bag in his other hand.

"At the embassy?" Désirée asked. Franz Stroheim, her nephew, though few knew it, was an Austrian diplomat.

"We dined together. We meet up every so often. We have ever since—""

"You and Raoul helped rescue his cousin's husband and your friend." Désirée pulled the door to behind them. "I wish—"

"You couldn't have." Tony set his bag down on the bench inside the door. "We can't risk anyone knowing we're together. Even O'Roarke, much as I trust him. And you could have ended up arrested and in the Conciergerie yourself."

"And made your life harder?"

"And put me in a panic." Tony hesitated, shifting Sophie against him as she snuggled. "Seeing what my friend and Franz's cousin faced drives it home. What you're risking every day."

Désirée reached out a hand to smooth Sophie's downy hair. "No one's actually tried to arrest me."

"That's because no one knows where you are."

"I can't imagine I'm of much interest." She wasn't going to tell Tony about the warnings she'd received from friends she was still in touch with.

"Don't sell yourself short, sweetheart."

She tugged Sophie's lace collar smooth. "I'm out of the game."

"No one's out of the game. You told me as much yourself."

"That was before Waterloo. Before I was a mother."

"You can't have it both ways, my love. No one's going to see you as a mother living quietly in the country. Even if you saw yourself that way. Which you don't."

"A point."

"And if you were, you wouldn't be regretting not having been able to help Franz and O'Roarke and me."

Désirée smiled at Sophie as their daughter grasped hold of her finger. "Sadly, you take that point as well."

"Of course we'd have been the better for your skills, but we managed. O'Roarke's got the Kestrel to help us."

"Yes, that impressed me."

Tony's gaze flickered across her face. "Do you—"

"Know who he is?" Désirée looked up from Sophie. "No comment."

A faint smile curved Tony's mouth.

"Did you have other help?" she asked, as they moved to the cushioned settee before the fireplace. One of her additions to the cottage. It hadn't been here that night Tony had bandaged her wound and she'd stolen the papers back from him. "I never asked but now that Barton and St. Georges are safely out of France it's hardly dangerous."

Tony hesitated as he settled himself beside her with Sophie. "O'Roarke got Mélanie Rannoch to help."

"That's good. She's quite brilliant. And I imagine she feels the need to take action as much as I do."

"I hadn't thought of it that way. I was concerned—"

"For her marriage? Malcolm Rannoch's very good at what he does, from what I've seen, but she and Raoul must be clever enough to keep it from him. She'll never be happy as a diplomatic wife."

Tony's brows drew together. "Call me a fool, but from what I've seen she loves her husband."

"Oh, I think she does. Quite desperately, I'd say." Once she'd have tossed those words off with irony, but it was easier to say them now. "And my guess is she's been genuinely trying to make it work after Waterloo. Without playing for the other side. But it's difficult to find happiness denying who you are." Désirée tilted her head back. "I'm grateful you've never asked me to do that."

"I wouldn't dare. But I also wouldn't want to."

"That's why I love you, Tony."

Tony shifted Sophie against his shoulder and pressed a kiss to her forehead. "I like Rannoch. I think he loves his wife. And I think he appreciates her."

"So do I." Désirée watched her lover with their daughter and had a similar image of Malcolm Rannoch holding his toddler son against his shoulder in Vienna. "But he doesn't know her. Not completely."

"Does anyone know anyone else completely?"

"God, I hope not. We should all have some privacy. But he knows her less than some. Because she can't be herself with him. Not completely." She had an image of Mélanie Rannoch at the sleighing party in Vienna. A vision in sugar-plum gauze and gold net. The perfect diplomatic wife. An impeccable performance. But still a performance.

Tony stroked his fingers over Sophie's sparse hair. "I was furious with O'Roarke when I realized what had happened."

"Understandable." Tony had always been more squeamish than she was about the compromises inherent in the espionage game. Whereas for her, the idea that Raoul had set a woman to spy on his son had evoked more admiration for his audacity than horror. At least then. Now it was Raoul who shot into Désirée's memory, that same night at the Schönbrunn Palace, watching Malcolm and Mélanie Rannoch. "Except that he's in love with her himself."

Tony's frown deepened.

"You must have seen it."

"No, I did. I couldn't decide if that made it better or worse."

"I'm not sure it's an either/or. But I don't think he's thinking entirely like a spymaster. Which could be a fault in and of itself. But perhaps not with you."

Tony grinned at Sophie as she tugged his cravat free of his waistcoat. "Meaning I've always tended to let feelings get in the way?"

"Do you deny it?"

"By no means. Where would we be if I hadn't?"

Désirée smiled at their daughter as Sophie tossed the end of the cravat in the air and giggled. "An excellent point, my love."

CHAPTER 12

June 1821
Sawden Park, Surrey

Lisette Varon drew her shawl about her shoulders and stared out across the rolling lawn towards the lake and the grotto and folly visible in the distance. Rustic charm laid out with exquisite taste and a great deal of expense. Candlelight from the salon behind spilt onto the stones of the terrace. The footmen had just finished lighting the candles. Most of the guests were still upstairs dressing for dinner, but soon they would gather in the salon. Désirée had made sure to outline the plan of the evening when Lisette and her mother and sister arrived. With the faint smile of one who wasn't used to this world sharing it with others who weren't either.

Lisette turned to Raoul, who, like her, had finished dressing early. As always, he was impeccably attired and looked totally at ease. Complicated as women's clothes could be, she'd always been grateful disguise didn't entail tying a cravat. "I never thought to be in a world like this. Well, not when I wasn't on a mission."

He raised his brows. "You grew up at Malmaison."

"My mother was a seamstress." Lisette smoothed the skirt of her gown. The azure silk flowers embroidered on the cream-colored gauze shimmered in the candlelight. Rosettes of azure ribbon frothed over her embroidered satin slippers. Having a mother who was a dressmaker had always been an asset when masquerading among the aristocracy. "I was observing this world growing up, not really part of it. Not like you. Or Mélanie."

"Mélanie would probably argue that she's not properly part of it now. And I've certainly never been."

Lisette regarded the man she had known as long as she could remember. Who had recruited her as an agent, to her mother's endless regret, though it had given Lisette a badly needed outlet. "You were born in this world, Raoul. I can play at it well enough. But I can't imagine *living* in it."

Raoul dug a shoulder into one of the stone pillars on the terrace. "It's a luxurious estate. But it's still an escape from the world in many ways. I think that's what Tony and Désirée want it to be."

"He'll always be a duke, though. He may not realize quite what that means, but I imagine Désirée does."

"I imagine she does. And she loves him despite it."

Lisette smiled. "They've found a way to be happy." She tucked her hands under her shawl. Lyons silk. A gift from the Empress Josephine. "I'm sorry I didn't tell you. About Franz." Franz Stroheim, Désirée's nephew. Who had become Lisette's friend and ally, though they were on opposite sides. Whom she suddenly felt unaccountably shy round. Perhaps because she could guess at the reasons she and her family had been included in the house party.

"There was no need to tell me," Raoul said. "Your personal life is your business."

"Well, this part of it involved another agent."

"That would only be relevant if you shared secrets with that agent."

"It was more the other way round. Though we were both careful. But Franz was the one struggling with where his loyalties lay."

"Yes. I saw that as far back as Vienna."

"It was part of what drew me to him. But I didn't want to be—I didn't want to be an excuse for him to betray his country or his family."

Raoul turned, leaning against the pillar, to face her directly. "I don't think Stroheim's the sort to change loyalties for personal reasons."

"No. He's much too thoughtful. It's more that I wanted to be sure he wasn't drawn to me simply because I was an excuse to change his loyalties, if that makes sense."

"It does indeed. But having seen you with Stroheim, I don't believe it for a moment."

"No." Lisette turned to him with a quick smile. "I believe that now." She gripped her elbows beneath the shawl. Above the long gloves that felt like someone else's skin. "But I can't see myself as an aristocrat's wife."

"I've seen you play the role of aristocrat to perfection."

"That's not it. I know the rules. But I'd go mad following them. Even as much as Mélanie does. Or Laura."

Raoul frowned. "You think Laura tries to follow rules?"

"Anyone who lives in the beau monde does, to a degree. It's the price of being part of that world. All of you have more freedom than most, but you still want to move in that world and that requires following certain rules. You can't tell me Laura doesn't make compromises at times. I mean, she grew up in it, so maybe she doesn't notice—"

"She grew up in India."

"As a colonel's daughter. And whatever you decide to do with your life now, she's going to want to make it possible for you."

"So I'm constraining Laura's choices by giving up being a spymaster?"

"I didn't mean that. I'm sure Laura's thrilled to have you home more. And safe. But I'm afraid I'd lose myself if—"

"You married Stroheim?"

Lisette's fingers tightened on the folds of her shawl. "He hasn't asked me."

"My dear. I hesitate to claim to know anyone else's mind. But I've seen the way he looks at you. And he's not a man to not want to marry the woman he loves."

Lisette felt herself color and glanced away. "Wives are expected to foster their husbands' careers. It's damnable."

"It is."

"But it's the way of the world. And for the moment we have to live with it. It's all very well to theorize about how the world should be and try to change it, but for the present we have to live in the world we have."

"The revolutionary's eternal dilemma."

She swiveled her neck to look back at him. "How do you do it?"

"I'm trying to put my life back together. I may stand for Parliament. And yes, I realize the strain that may put on Laura. I'll try to make sure Laura doesn't think that means she has to behave a certain way. And yes, I realize she probably will anyway."

"I wasn't trying to be difficult."

"You were sharing keen insights. Which I profoundly hope is what I've always asked you to do."

Lisette glanced at the house where the guests would soon assemble. "I see Mélanie. Trying to make sure she does what Malcolm needs to succeed in Parliament. Sometimes against her instincts, I think."

She saw memories shoot through Raoul's mind. Moments from Vienna and Brussels and Paris, she suspected. "I think Malcolm's trying to make sure Mélanie realizes she doesn't have to."

"So do I. But I also think she's doing it more than he realizes."

"I won't argue with that. And you also think Laura would?"

"That's between you and Laura."

Raoul hesitated. "We change. Because of relationships. Inevitably, being connected with other people changes us. I don't know that I'd say that's a bad thing. I'm certainly not the man I was before I met Laura."

"And you've changed even more since."

"Because I'm a father. That is, I changed when Malcolm was born, but being able to openly be a father changed me. A change I perhaps recognized all too late. But the real challenge would be if it were a change I couldn't bear to make. In the end, it was a change I needed to make for myself. Or at least, wanted to."

"Which gets back to the challenge. We all want the people we love to be happy. How does one know when the change is outside what one wants?" She watched him for a moment. "Do you have regrets?"

"My dear. I live with regrets every day of my life. But about this—no. Or no, that's not quite it. How could I not, at moments? But in the end, I think it was the right choice. I think of what I've gained, not what I've lost. I think perhaps that's the key."

Lisette watched him closely. He was still pale, but his gaze held an ease she had rarely seen. "You look happy."

"Oh, I've been happy for a long time. I'm frequently not sure if I deserve it. But I'm still happy." He smiled at her. "I quite recommend it. It can be complicated. But it certainly beats the alternative."

Lisette smiled. "I never saw myself married. It worked for my parents, even if we didn't have Papa long enough. It seems it works for friends—the Rannochs, the Davenports. Julien, to my shock. I see it work for you—"

"You encouraged me to believe it could. When I was all too inclined to believe the opposite."

"Well, I knew you." She thought back to the moment in Paris she'd gone to a jeweler with him to buy earrings for his lover, whose name she still hadn't known. "I knew if you cared about someone that much, it must be special. And I knew you'd do everything you could to make it work. And I suppose by that time"—she colored again but did not look away—"I was thinking about Franz. I was imagining what could be possible. Even if I couldn't quite see it for myself, I could imagine it for someone else. I didn't want you to lose that."

"Generous. But I'd advise you to be generous with yourself as well. You certainly deserve it."

"Don't you always say it would be a hard world if we all got what we deserved?"

"Perhaps when it comes to me. Certainly not when it comes to you. You deserve nothing but happiness. And whatever you decide that means, I'll try to help you find it."

CHAPTER 13

"Champagne before dinner. A delightful idea," Kitty took a sip from her glass. "I think I'll adopt it."

The salon was filling with the dinner guests. Crystal clinked. Désirée had had the footmen pour champagne. Mélanie quite agreed with Kitty and thought she might copy it as well. She turned from speaking with Cordelia and Kitty to see Franz Stroheim leaning against the wall, gaze on Lisette, who was talking with Laura, as though he wanted to cross to her but wasn't sure of his welcome.

Mélanie excused herself to Cordelia and Kitty and went to his side. "Your aunt is an excellent hostess."

Franz grinned and glanced at Désirée, who was talking to Raoul and John Wilcox. "I think she'd be excellent at anything she put her hand to. Though I'm sure this was a life she never envisioned."

"Many of us don't."

"No." Stroheim took a drink of champagne. "Vienna seems a long way away."

"Centuries and centuries." Mélanie lifted her glass to his.

"I remember the night we met. At Julie Zichy's. And then talking at the sleighing party."

"So do I. I was terrified of you."

He laughed. "I can't imagine anyone being terrified of me. Especially when you first met me. I was a callow youth."

"You were anything but callow. And I was terrified you guessed the truth about me. I think I was right."

His gaze narrowed. "Not at first. I just was quite sure I'd seen you at Josephine's. I even wondered if you'd been a British agent. I'd heard the stories of your work with Malcolm. I thought you might have been undercover then."

"Instead of my being undercover when you met me."

"I did start to wonder. In Vienna, and later in Paris. Oh, you never did anything to give yourself away. In fact, you were so convincing that even as I began to have suspicions, I'd doubt myself. But by the time O'Roarke helped Tony and me rescue Barton and St. Georges from the Conciergerie, I had a fairly shrewd notion of where O'Roarke's true loyalties lay. I knew he was friendly with you and Malcolm. Neither of you ever gave anything away—but sometimes one has an instinct about such things."

Mélanie took a drink of champagne. "You're a frightening man, Franz. As I knew then."

"But I wouldn't have done anything. I was confused about who knew what, but I knew you and Malcolm cared for each other. And I was already questioning my own loyalties." He drew a breath, gaze fixed across the lawn outside the French windows in the twilight shadows. "And wondering about how those loyalties impacted personal relationships."

"Such as loving someone on the opposite side?"

He met her gaze. "I wasn't sure which side I was on. But I knew how I felt about Lisette." He risked a quick glance at Lisette, who had been joined by her mother and sister, then looked back at Mélanie. "I wasn't sure how she felt about me. Especially during the hundred days, and after Waterloo. I knew what I wanted. But I knew she'd only be happy with me if she could be true to herself. And I wasn't even sure how to be true to myself."

"I'm not sure any of us is sure how to do that. Even if Polonius makes it sound ridiculously easy."

Franz glanced at Raoul, who was laughing with Désirée, then met Mélanie's gaze. "When I worked out the truth about O'Roarke, I admired him. Standing for something without getting caught up worrying about countries."

"He rather tends to bring out admiration. Though he'd be the first to say he's compromised as much as anyone. He'd also probably say it's impossible not to do so. That loyalty is a matter of choices. One often can't be true to every loyalty at once."

"God, yes. I knew that before Waterloo. I can't remember when I didn't know it, really." Stroheim shifted his shoulders against the wall. His gaze moved back to Lisette, who had her arm round her younger sister Minette. "She's loyal to France. More than I ever was to Austria, if it comes to that. But she's happy here."

"And you're wondering if you could be?"

"Oh, I think I could be happy anywhere—" He drew in his breath.

"Where Lisette was?"

"Does that make me sound a foolish romantic?"

"On the contrary. I think I could be happy anywhere Malcolm was. It was hard to be at home in Britain, though." She could say that to Franz. She couldn't say it to Malcolm. Or even Cordy or Harry.

"But you are now?"

She hesitated a moment. She wasn't sure she'd ever actually said it. Even to herself, "I think so. It's my children's home."

Franz nodded. "I asked her," he said. "After Waterloo. I asked her to marry me." The words came out quickly and Mélanie had a sense he hadn't admitted this to anyone. "She accused me of only doing it to protect her, but that wasn't it. I mean, I did want to protect her, of course, but that's because I love her. She said she couldn't leave France and her comrades. And that she was needed, and she couldn't be the wife of an Austrian diplomat and help former Bonapartists evade the French authorities—" He broke off.

"She could, actually," Mélanie said. "I can say that from experience. But she's right that it would have challenged her conscience."

Franz met her gaze, his own open and direct. "You helped when we were getting Barton and St. Georges out of the Conciergerie, didn't you?"

Mélanie felt herself smile, though it had once been a secret she'd danced on a knife's point to protect. "We tried so hard to keep it from you."

"I told you, I wasn't sure of anything."

"I wouldn't let Raoul keep me out of it. But he wouldn't let me do anything that involved you directly. I'd given up spying by that time. But I wasn't going to stand by with my friends in danger. It wasn't the first time or the last. Lisette wouldn't have been able to stay on the sidelines either."

"No. She said as much. I love her for it. And she said I wouldn't love her if she changed. Which I don't think is true, but I'd hate myself if she changed for me. So we agreed. We both had to work for our countries, and that meant we couldn't be together, at least not for the moment. And then she had to flee France, and I only got a brief letter. We wrote. So much we couldn't say, but a lot we did. So many times I had the impulse to simply sail for Britain. But it's difficult to walk away from one's life. Even a life one is doubting."

"So it is," Mélanie said.

He shot a look at her.

"I was torn about being an agent. Torn in two, at times. But it was also difficult to stop. I'd have been letting down people. And myself."

Stroheim nodded. "Then I had a chance to bring Désirée and

Sophie to Britain. They needed me. Just as I was truly at the breaking point with my old life. And I'm not sure—"

"That you want to go back?"

He met her gaze. "I'd stay if Lisette wanted me to. I suppose I'm afraid to ask. Because if she says no, I've lost my reason for staying. I've lost my anchor, in a way."

"I can understand that."

"Can you?"

"I lived with uncertainty with Malcolm for years. Afraid that if he learnt the truth about me our relationship would be over. Hard as it was to keep the secret, the alternative seemed worse."

"That's how you were in Paris."

"And when we first came to Britain. But in the end, we got through it. And Lisette is much likelier to accept you than Malcolm was to forgive me."

Stroheim gave a faint smile and glanced at Lisette as she turned to talk to Harry. "I hope so."

SYLVIE CROSSED the salon to Julien. He had been talking to Toby Ludgrove, who had just moved away. Caught. He'd used to be better at armoring himself against Sylvie.

Sylvie's smile said she knew she'd caught him unawares. "It seems we'll be seeing each other more." She tilted her head to one side, blonde ringlets dancing over diamond eardrops. "You seem to have become a friend of Papa Duke and his new duchess. And he and Mama Duchess seem to have decided that the world can be well lost for love after all." She glanced from Tony and Désirée to Hetty and John Wilcox. "Of course, all of them have their creature comforts seen to. Nothing like living in luxury to make it easier to survive scandal."

"I can imagine the frustration," Julien said.

She shot a look at him over the gilded rim of her champagne glass. "Can you?"

"Seeing people escape marriages."

"Oh, don't worry. I've never emulated my in-laws' example and I'm not planning to start now. In any case, Oliver wouldn't want to leave Isobel, and even if he did, we'd likely only make each other miserable." Sylvie had parted from her first love years ago, but she'd never really been over him for all her protestations that it wouldn't have worked. As Sylvie herself said, they should have had a chance to try. "But I am—intrigued—to put it mildly—to see the careful strictures I've been compelled to live my life by so lightly tossed aside by the older generation. It would almost be amusing if I weren't in the midst of it. St. Ives isn't happy about it, but then he hates seeing the settled order of his life disrupted. Rosy's the one who threw a tantrum." Sylvie cast a quick glance at her youngest sister-in-law, who was talking to Raoul, a hectic flush mantling her cheeks. "But then she's terribly conventional for all of her sophistication and her genuine abilities as an agent."

"It's one thing to flout convention oneself. It's another to see one's parents do it."

Sylvie gave a short laugh. "Why did you come here, Julien?"

"Isn't it obvious?" Julien dug his shoulder into the frame of a French window. "To support our friends."

"You never do anything for such a simple reason."

"Why did you come here?"

"Isn't it obvious? Because Papa Duke and Mama Duchess decreed it."

"You never do anything for such a simple reason."

"Family are complicated."

"Still. You can't tell me you can't wrap St. Ives round your finger. Or simply defy him."

"We've never had the same power, Julien. You have a title. I married one."

"Succinctly put."

"I've never been free."

"Which doesn't change the question—who are you working for now?" Julien asked.

"Usually you're subtler than this."

"Do I really need to be subtle? We're old friends, after all."

"Is that what people are calling it now?"

"There are any number of words for it. But that encompasses a lot. You've known me longer than almost anyone in this room."

"You're the one who deduced I'm working for Castlereagh."

"And you admitted it far too readily. There's someone else."

"Now you're talking like a jealous lover."

"Never. But you've never been one for any sort of fidelity. You've always seen the advantages of keeping your options open."

"You can't imagine anyone I might be working for would care about a family house party. I'm stuck here."

"I can't imagine your being stuck anywhere."

"My dear." Sylvie tossed down a deep swallow of champagne. "I've been stuck since I became Lady St. Ives. What else is marriage?"

CHAPTER 14

"I saw the children making themselves at home." Tony smiled at Mélanie, who was seated on his left at the long dinner table.

"What could be better than a ruined castle for the imagination?" Mélanie took a drink of Bordeaux. The wine was superb, as was the food, and the conversation was flowing quite easily, but she could feel the tension running round the table as though the wax tapers had sparked lightning.

"We used to act out fairy tales in it," Helena said. "Do you remember Cinderella, Freddie?"

"How could I forget." Frederica set her fork down. They had abandoned the strictures of formal dinners and were talking generally round the table. "I had to be the stepmother."

"Funny it never occurred to us then we'd actually have a step-mother one day," Rosalind said.

Helena quickly turned her gaze to her elder brother. "We made St. Ives be the prince."

"Good god, I'd forgot." St. Ives set his glass down. "We weren't here that much. It was mostly Father's house."

"It was a family house, hopefully," Tony said.

"Were we a family?" Rosalind asked.

"There are many different definitions of family, my dear," Hetty said. "But I hope we'll always be one."

"It was my favorite house as a boy." Tony leant back in his chair. "What always intrigued me most was the buried treasure."

"You mean all those old stories?" Rosalind asked. "Are they really true?"

"Oh yes." Tony reached for a walnut and cracked it. "You should have listened more to my attempts at history lessons. It goes back to the Civil War. O'Roarke will appreciate that."

"Ludlow's a favorite of mine," Malcolm said.

"Mine too," Raoul said. "Lessons on recovering from a loss."

"Yes, well, this was before Parliament's loss," Tony said. "During the Civil War, the Viscount St. Ives—it was before the dukedom—fought with the Royalists. Lady St. Ives and the children sought refuge at Sawden. But parliamentary forces occupied it. They also took much of the family's plate and jewels. But Lady St. Ives hid away the ancestral jewels. A magnificent set of emeralds. You can see her wearing them in her painting on the stair wall. Later the whole family fled to France. They returned under Charles II, and St. Ives was created Duke of Bamford. But the jewels were never recovered. One story was that Lady St. Ives—the new duchess—disliked her daughter-in-law, whom their son had married in France, and didn't want her to have them."

"That's always sounded likely to me," Sylvie said. "Her daughter-in-law was French. She probably thought of her as a usurper."

"It fascinated us from when we were children," Tony said. "One reason I always loved Sawden. We'd go treasure hunting every chance we got."

"And you really never found them?" Helena asked.

"Don't you think they'd be on display if I had?"

"Not necessarily. Then they'd just be ordinary jewels instead of treasure."

"Excellent thinking, my dear," Tony said. "But no, I really never did. The treasure is still there for the hunting."

"Is that a challenge?" Laura asked. She was seated on Tony's right.

"Take it how you will. My father used to accuse us children of being too obsessed with the story, and say the Southcott jewels must have been dug up years ago or it was all a hum. But I never believed him."

"Fathers want to take all the fun out of things," Julien said. "That is the prior generation. I'd never do anything of the sort."

"Remember some fathers of the prior generation are at table," Raoul said.

"You don't count," Julien said. "You're an agreeable father. Who set the tone for the rest of us. So is Tony."

"You never mentioned the jewels." Percy Rawdon looked down the table at his wife.

"Didn't I?" Frederica said. "Well, we haven't come to Sawden often and it wasn't the sort of thing I thought about so much when I was properly grown up. One forgets."

"One gets sadly dull," Helena said. "It takes being here with the children to recapture that. There's a secret passage, too. We used to love to run through it."

"Lord, I'd almost forgot," Frederica said. "In those days I didn't care about the cobwebs in my hair."

"There were always rumors we had a secret Catholic in the family because of the passage," Tony said. "But the truth is I think one of the earls built it to smuggle his mistress in and out of the house."

"We have one like that at Dunmykel," Malcolm said. "There are reasons I was drawn to study history."

Tony flashed a grin at him.

"And to think I thought it was our childhood rambles." Raoul took a drink of wine.

"Those helped too. Of course, I think you were the first one who told me about the scandals at Dunmykel and the secret passage."

Raoul grinned. "There are all sorts of ways to make history engaging. Scandals are one of the best."

~

"Tony and Désirée managed that remarkably well." Mélanie unwrapped her shawl from her shoulders and draped it over a chairback in the pretty bedchamber they'd been allotted. "And to think I ever thought any of our family dinners was fraught."

"It's a challenging thing they're doing," Malcolm said. "I want to do everything we can to help them succeed. Of course, it helps that they're—"

"Besotted?"

"At least Bamford is."

"I think she is too." Mélanie untied the ribbons on her slippers and stepped out of them. "In her way. In fact, I'd say she adores him. Even if she can't quite admit it to herself. Or perhaps she can now. But she probably needs to keep some of herself distinct."

"It's not easy. As we know." His hands froze unwinding his cravat. "Not that—"

"Darling?" Mélanie looked at her husband. "We never really talked about it, but watching Tony and Désirée can't but stir thoughts."

"Well, yes." Malcolm tossed the cravat after her shawl. "I'm wondering what would have happened if we'd met and I'd known you were a spy. Could you imagine it?"

"What?" Mélanie unclasped her peridot necklace and set it down on the dressing table.

"What Tony and Désirée did for years. Having an affair in bits and pieces when we could snatch time together."

"Yes." She aligned the links of the necklace. The green stones flashed in the light of the tapers on the dressing table. Scenes from the past, reframed, flickered through her memory. Lisbon, Vienna, Brussels, Paris. What if they'd been engaged in an open battle of wits instead of her keeping secrets. "Though I think it would have bothered you."

"Not really." Malcolm undid his shirt cuffs. "I've always had friends who were French agents. I don't think you'd have been able to leave off trying to get information from me, though."

Mélanie unhooked an earring and watched the peridot dangle from her fingertips. "Would you?"

"What?"

"Have been able to leave off trying to get information from me?"

"I"—he gave her an abashed smile—"I'm not sure."

"Good answer." She put the earring in its box and unhooked its mate.

"It would have depended on what it was. And what our agreement was. I can't see your agreeing not to take anything from me." He undid another button. "I mean, we haven't really agreed to that now, have we?"

"We've agreed we can't foresee all the exceptions."

"Precisely." Malcolm glanced down at his shirt cuff. "Poor devil."

"Who?" Mélanie tugged at the strings on her embroidered tulle overdress.

"Bamford. Married to the duchess all those years when he'd have been much happier with Désirée Clairineau. This should put an end to any nonsense you've thought about what would have happened if I'd married an English girl."

Mélanie started to speak, and bit back her words. Because it was true the vague image of a girl Malcolm might have been happy with had haunted her for years. Still did, on occasion. The Duke and Duchess of Bamford had never appeared unhappy precisely, but that was not the marriage she had envisioned for Malcolm. And it would have driven Malcolm mad even more than Bamford.

"I'd just have met you later and gone through a divorce," Malcolm added.

Mélanie choked.

"I'd have loved you, you know. Anywhere, under any circumstance. It just would have been more awkward in some circumstances."

Mélanie stepped out of the cloud of peach-embroidered tulle. "More awkward than what we had?"

"Oh yes. We were married and had the leisure of getting to know each other before we had to confront being on opposite sides. Well, before I did."

"Oh, darling." Mélanie walked up to him and put her arms round him. "You put things like no one else."

Malcolm slid his own arms round her. "Can you deny any of it?"

"Well, I'd put it a bit differently."

"That's because you're too hard on yourself."

"You think I should take lessons from Désirée?"

"I'm not sure. I think she has more qualms than she lets on."

"Yes, so do I, actually. She doesn't let herself dwell on regrets. It doesn't mean she doesn't have them. In fact, I suspect she's too honest to deny that she has them." Mélanie frowned. "It's not easy."

He slid his hands up her back. "Being married agents?"

"Joining the beau monde."

"They aren't, really. Lucky them."

"Not yet. But they're on the edges of it. It's hard to stay away. We know that."

"Maybe they're stronger than we are."

Mélanie laughed. "I like them."

"So do I. I like Lisette and Stroheim, too."

"Yes, so do I. I mean, you know I'm fond of Lisette, and I

always liked Franz. Even when I was afraid he guessed the truth about me."

"I saw you talking to him before dinner."

"He admitted he's in love with Lisette. He wants to propose but he's afraid she'll say no."

"He told you a lot."

"He needed to talk to a friend. Which I suppose I am, rather to my surprise."

Malcolm watched her for a moment in the flickering candle-light. "Were you—"

Mélanie stared at him. "Malcolm, for god's sake, I didn't meet Stroheim until we were married."

Malcolm returned her gaze. "And you were spying on me. And Stroheim could have had useful information. And you needed to learn more about him."

"But I wasn't—I really didn't, Malcolm. You do believe that, don't you?"

"Yes, actually. It would have been a risk, for one thing. Though in the right circumstances—you've said yourself fidelity didn't mean anything to you then."

"I'd have told you. After. When you knew the rest." She put her hands on his shoulders. "I know it sounds absurd, but there'd been enough lies."

"I thought we agreed we'd always need to lie to each other about some things."

"But not that."

"Fair enough." He folded his arms. "I'm not sure why, though. Especially since it didn't mean anything to you at that point. Why was it a line you were so careful about?"

"Because it mattered to you. And yes, I know I crossed every sort of line. But sometimes one has to hold on to certain things. That must sound insane—"

"No, I think I understand."

"Also—it probably meant something to me before I admitted it did."

The corner of his mouth lifted in a smile. "That sounds so lovely I'll let myself believe it."

"You know me, Malcolm. I'd never make up such a sentimental lie."

He grinned. "You have me there, sweetheart."

CHAPTER 15

*J*ulien sat up in bed, all senses alert. Kitty pushed herself up beside him. No need to ask if she'd heard it too. They were both always keyed to the smallest sound, whether camping in the underbrush listening for snipers or sleeping in palaces listening for intrigue. Or sleeping anywhere, listening for the sound of a child, as he'd learnt more recently. Neither of them slept well.

Light, crisp footfalls sounded in the passage. "Sylvie." He pushed back the covers. "I'd know those footsteps anywhere." He cast a glance at Kitty. "Sorry, but it's true."

"No need to apologize. Or explain."

"I suspect Désirée had her reasons for putting us next to her. Though not the reasons people might have placed Sylvie and me close together in the past." Julien scrambled into the shirt and breeches he'd draped over the footboard. Without quite admitting it, he'd known it was likely to come to this.

Kitty was up and had pulled a loose gown over her head. After what had happened to Raoul, none of them was likely to go into even the mildest danger without backup. Or to let a loved one do so. Julien grabbed a lamp and lit it, then reached back for his wife's hand.

They slipped out into the shadowy passage. Smooth polished floorboards and a discreet carpet down the center. The mullioned window at the end of the passage let in a shaft of moonlight. He'd always liked a full moon. Earlier in the night he'd been grateful for the way the light shone over Kitty's face and lit her amber hair and caught the flash of delight in her eyes. But that same pale glow now was just as helpful on a mission.

Kitty nodded towards faint indentations in the carpet. Even satin slippers left a tread. Foolish of Sylvie. But then she probably hadn't expected them to wake. Of course it was always possible Sylvie was just doing what would be expected of most people slipping from their bed at a house party. Visiting another bed. But this was Sylvie. And given the make-up of the guest list, he couldn't quite imagine whose bed she might be visiting. Percy? That would be interesting, but Sylvie's tastes had always run in a more sophisticated direction. And he couldn't see what she'd have to gain from it.

They followed the trail to the stairhead. Down the oak stairs, past the wainscoted walls with paintings of Bamfords past—for Tony's sake, Julien hoped he was happier with his ancestors than Julien was with his own; at Carfax Court paintings by his and Kitty's friends had replaced many Mallinsons past.

The lamplight only caught faint scuffs on the wooden boards of the stairs. But in the hall below, beneath the Bamford arms and the crossed swords, footprints showed in the Axminster rug. Towards the library.

Julien opened one of the double doors and lifted the lamp. The gilded magnificence of the library stretched before them. Not the duke's main library, but probably a beloved collection as this was one of his favorite houses. Shadows slid over the writing desks and groupings of sofas and chairs scattered about the room. The fireplace they could have walked inside with a painting of a prior duchess, probably Tony's mother, over it.

And at the far end of the room, in the orderly ranks of bookshelves, one out of place, revealing a shadowy gap.

"The secret passage," Julien murmured. "It almost seems like a cliché, but I suppose we should have known."

They moved across the room to the open panel to the passage. He stopped to scan the writing desk he'd seen the duke use, but there was no sign Sylvie had disrupted anything.

He lifted the lamp higher and nudged the panel further open. What on earth was Sylvie after? Or perhaps a better question was what did Bamford have hidden here that Sylvie was after. Or whom was she meeting?

Julien tightened his grip on Kitty's hand and stepped into the passage. Musty air. Dust that tickled the nose. Close stone walls. He and Kitty picked their way over the uneven ground with careful steps.

Light flickered against the stone as the passage snaked. A gasp sounded ahead. They rounded a bend and came upon a widened space lit by a torch flickering in the wall, casting warm light on the rough stone.

Sylvie, wrapped in a dark blue silk dressing gown, knelt in the dust, staring into a crevice in the wall.

"Looking for something?" Julien asked.

She swirled her head round to stare up at him, less surprised than frustrated. "It's gone."

"What is?" Kitty asked.

"The Bamford treasure."

"You knew where it was?" Kitty asked.

"Well, yes. But I wouldn't have been so interested in it if Papa Duke hadn't kept his papers with it. He'd never admit it, but he found the treasure ages ago and decided to use the hiding place."

Julien crouched down beside her. "I'm not sure whether to ask how you know or why you care?"

Sylvie's familiar gaze locked on his own. "I'm part of this family. Surely you don't have to ask how I know. As to why I care —I wouldn't have until recently. But they're letters between him and that woman. And I need to know her secrets."

"Why?"

"Why?" Sylvie's eyes flared open. "Because secrets are the currency of power." She drew a breath. "And because I think she betrayed my cousin Edouard. Who was a Royalist agent and was betrayed and killed after Waterloo."

"Given that Désirée was a Bonapartist agent, that's not precisely a betrayal."

"Surely that depends upon one's perspective."

"I suppose everything depends upon perspective."

"What were you planning to do with these papers?" Kitty asked.

"Expose her." Sylvie's eyes flared, molten lava that hardened to onyx. "All her crimes through the years. She lost at Waterloo. But she's going to be duchess. Duchess of Bamford."

"Which you thought you were for twenty-hour hours when we thought Tony was dead," Julien said. "Don't worry, you will be someday. If you live long enough and St. Ives doesn't decide to follow his parents' example."

"Darling." Kitty gripped Julien's arm. "That's not helping."

"Perhaps not, but it's satisfying." Julien kept his gaze on Sylvie. "And true."

Kitty looked at Sylvie. "Désirée and Tony are going to be a scandal. She may have the title duchess, but she'll hardly have the position your mother-in-law had. Nor does she want it."

"The beau monde have a way of changing. Some people remain on the outside forever. But others worm their way in. She's the sort that worms her way in. She may be lethal, but she's also the sort who can charm anyone. It was one thing when she was Papa Duke's mistress. But now she's going to be duchess and Mama Duchess won't fight her for any of it. I'm supposed to stand by and watch her have the name and the estates and the jewels and everything—"

"Everything you gave up the love of your life for," Kitty said.

Sylvie's eyes narrowed. "I didn't say that."

"No. I did." Kitty's gaze was steady in the shifting light.

Sylvie shrugged. "I don't use words like that. Anyway, Hubert pushed me to give up Oliver. But yes. That's what I was supposed to get. The supposed reward for everything I've put up with. She's going to have it and we're all going to be a scandal, and if they weather it, which I think they will, she'll get all the attention."

"You're being petty, Sylvie," Julien said.

"Since when am I not?"

"It depends. But your motives aside, the question would seem to be who took the jewels and the papers. And which were they after."

"And what other secrets do the papers contain," Kitty said.

"You want to protect her," Sylvie said.

"For the moment, I think we all want to recover what's lost," Julien said.

MÉLANIE CAME AWAKE with a jerk and sat up. Something was wrong. One of the children? No. No sound from the nursery. Berowne shifted on her feet and regarded her with a reproachful green eye that glittered in the dark. "Sorry." She reached out to pet him.

Malcolm pushed himself up beside her. "You heard it too?"

"Yes."

A creak. A door. Footsteps.

"Could be harmless intrigue," Malcolm said. "But given the guests at the house party—"

"Quite." Mélanie snatched up the seafoam silk slip she had

worn to dinner with her tulle overdress and pulled it over her head.

Malcolm scrambled into a shirt and breeches and lit a candle. Mélanie grabbed the candle, tugged open the nursery door, and glanced inside, Berowne winding round her ankles. All was quiet, the children snuggled two abed in the cane-work beds. Jessica stretched and rolled over next to Drusilla, arm round her stuffed cat. Mélanie eased the door closed and followed Malcolm out into the passage. It stretched long and shadowy. A creak sounded from downstairs. Malcolm seized her hand and they picked their way down the passage, past the paintings along the broad wooden stairs, across the high-ceilinged hall, and out the front door.

The night air bit through her slip. She should have grabbed a shawl, though it only would have been one more thing to hold on to. Moonlight washed over the lawn. A shadowy form was making his way across the lawn towards the stables. Of one accord she and Malcolm ran. The figure cast a quick glance over his shoulder, face a blur, then started to run.

CHAPTER 16

*M*alcolm sprinted and sprang at the fleeing figure. They thudded to the ground and landed in a tangle. The figure scrambled to his feet and started to run, then screamed as a streak of gray shot across the grass and leapt onto his legs.

"Berowne." Mélanie ran after Malcolm, their quarry, and their cat, who must have slipped out of the bedroom after them.

"Get this damned thing off me." The voice was unmistakably Percy Rawdon.

"Rawdon." Malcolm grabbed Berowne by the back of the neck. Berowne must have dug his claws in because Percy screamed. By the time Mélanie reached the men, Malcolm was holding a squirming Berowne and Percy was clutching his leg. "I think that monster drew blood."

"It's odd. He's usually very friendly. But he does have strong opinions." Mélanie took Berowne from Malcolm. Berowne settled against her chest and started to purr.

Malcolm regarded Percy, who was fully dressed, and glanced towards the stables where Percy had been headed. "Where do you think you're going?"

"Why should I want to stay here?" Percy straightened up, wincing at the pull on his leg. "Cursed dull in the country, and it's positively indecent how the duke and duchess and their lovers are carrying on. Freddie and I never should have brought the children here."

"So you're leaving without them?" Mélanie asked.

"Couldn't insist Freddie leave her parents' house, and she wouldn't send the children off with me."

"So, you're what? Trying to make a moral statement?" Malcolm asked. "By leaving in the middle of the night?"

"Shouldn't have to justify my actions to you, Rannoch. Don't see why I'm not free to do as I choose. Including leaving whenever I choose and going wherever I choose. For that matter—"

He broke off as footsteps thudded over the lawn. From the direction of the folly. Julien, Kitty, and Sylvie came running towards them.

"Where the devil did you come from?" Percy demanded.

"The folly," Kitty said.

"Having a midnight picnic?" Percy's gaze shot from Julien, in an untucked shirt and breeches, to Kitty, in a muslin shift, to Sylvie, barefoot, wrapped in a blue silk dressing gown.

"The secret passage opens onto it." Julien took a step towards Percy. "But then I expect you know that."

"Why should I know that?"

"Just a hunch." Julien looked from Percy to Sylvie. "What a good thing we're all here. You should both know better than to go exploring with so many spies in the house."

"Oh, go back to bed, Julien," Sylvie said. "This is a family matter."

"Can't wait to be free of this place," Percy said. "And as I was telling Rannoch, I have every right to leave."

"So you do. But not to take anything with you." Julien jerked Percy's coat from his shoulders and shook it on the ground. A series of objects thudded to the grass. Emeralds and tarnished

97

gold gleamed in the moonlight. A necklace, a tiara, a bracelet, earrings.

"You took the Southcott jewels," Sylvie said.

Percy straightened his shoulders. "I was curious after Bamford's story at dinner."

"You mean you wanted the jewels," Sylvie said.

"Who wouldn't want to uncover treasure from two centuries ago?"

"So you'll put it in a museum," Julien suggested.

"It belongs in the family."

"It belongs with Papa Duke," Sylvie said. "But never mind. Just give me the papers."

"What papers?"

"They should have been in the chest with the jewels. Papa Duke hid his letters to Désirée. I've always wondered where. I realized that tonight he might have put them with the treasure."

"But he said no one had discovered it," Percy said.

"Oh, he said that. But since when does he tell the truth about everything?"

"Why would he lie about this?"

"To keep his hiding place."

"But—"

"Oh, for heaven's sake, Percy. You found the jewels. Do you really think an accomplished agent couldn't? He must have thought he was terribly clever using a hiding place that had worked for nearly two hundred years. Though I suspect he'll feel considerably less clever knowing you stumbled across it."

"Well, you can look at the chest if you want. It's in my room. But I looked carefully and there aren't any papers in it. I'm leaving for London." Percy took a step towards the stables, a regretful eye on the jewels.

"I assume you somehow planned to circle back by the house and return the missing Southcott jewels to the duke on your way off the property?" Julien said.

Percy flushed in the cool light. "Absurd to leave those lying about. They belong somewhere safe. Somewhere we know where they are."

"I suppose you could argue if you sold them to a London jeweler you'd know where they were," Julien said. "Although before long they'd have to be taken apart and sold off and then you wouldn't have the least idea where they were."

"You have no proof I meant to do anything of the sort."

"Depends on what one means by proof," Julien said as Malcolm and Kitty gathered up the jewels. "By your own admission you were on your way off the property and you had the jewels with you."

"This isn't your affair, Carfax. Or Lady Carfax's. Or Rannoch's or Mrs. Rannoch's. The jewels belong to the family. I'm a member of the family."

"The same family you were just disparaging as so wracked by scandal you were compelled to leave the house?" Mélanie shifted Berowne against her shoulder. He was soft and boneless now but she wasn't taking any chances.

"And I'm a member of the family." Sylvie folded her arms.

"You can't expect me to want them to fall into the hands of a dangerous foreign agent like Désirée Clairineau," Percy said. "You can't want that either."

"You mean the future Duchess of Bamford?" Malcolm picked up an earring. "Perhaps it's a failure of imagination, but I don't see what she could do with these that would be a threat to British interests."

"But she would look quite stunning in them," Julien said. "For the moment, I think we'd all like to find the papers."

"I wouldn't," Percy said. "Couldn't care less what Bamford wrote to his mistress."

Malcolm looked at the earrings and tiara in his hands. "We'll return these to Bamford."

"Never were his," Percy said. "They belong to ancestors he

doesn't take seriously."

"How did you find them?" Mélanie asked. "I must say it's quite impressive, given they've been lost for so long."

"What? Oh, made sense it might be in this passage Freddie and Helena were talking about." Percy brightened at the praise. "So I decided to explore it tonight. Couldn't sleep; thought I might as well have a look."

"And you just happened to discover the secret hiding place?" Mélanie asked.

"Yes." Percy took a step towards her, then backed up as Berowne lifted his head. "That is—er—the panel was ajar when I passed it in the secret passage. Almost missed it at first—"

"Of course you did," Sylvie said.

"But then I noticed and managed to pry it open. Someone else must have been there earlier—"

"The person who took the papers," Sylvie said.

"Very likely. Not my concern." Percy harrumphed and straightened his shoulders. "You have the jewels, Carfax. Or rather, Lady Carfax and Rannoch do. I assume I can trust you to return them to the duke. I'm off to London."

"Not so fast." Malcolm caught his arm.

"I beg your pardon, Rannoch. On what authority—"

"We're agents," Julien said, moving to grip Percy's other arm. "We're used to acting without authority. There are more of us than of you. And all things considered, I would think you'd rather face the duke now than have us follow you to London and bring you up before a magistrate."

Tony glanced round the group gathered in the salon. He was barefoot, wrapped in a dressing gown, as was Désirée. Only two lamps and the moonlight spilling through the French windows lit the room. All those involved in the midnight escapes were present. And Raoul, whom Malcolm had woken along with Tony and Désirée.

"You're saying there were no papers in this"—Tony held up the box the jewels had been in, which they'd retrieved from Percy's room—"when you found it?"

"You're admitting there were papers in it?" Sylvie asked.

Tony regarded his daughter-in-law. "There seems little point in denying that now."

"I didn't find it," Sylvie said. "If I had and there'd been papers, I wouldn't have mentioned them at all."

"That, I believe," Tony said. He looked at Percy.

"What would I have wanted with papers?" Percy asked, as though aggrieved that Tony had complicated his theft.

"What indeed." Tony surveyed his son-in-law across the salon. Like a particularly loathsome worm that is revealed to be even more loathsome. Save that Mélanie suspected Tony was far more tolerant of worms. "I will say this, Percy. You aren't a bore. I'm continually surprised by the lengths to which you will go."

"You're a fine one to talk, Bamford. You've brought a French agent to Britain."

Tony controlled an instinctive flinch. "My dear Percy. You can't believe there aren't a number of French agents in Britain. Former Bonapartist agents and those presently working for the Royalist government. Every country has agents."

"You know what I mean. I suppose it's none of my business if you want to marry your mistress and mire the family in scandal. But surely you don't want to make the scandal worse by miring the family in charges of treason?"

Tony's fingers curled inwards. "Whom are you suggesting committed treason? If that's meant to be a slur against Désirée, the only person she could have committed treason against is Napoleon Bonaparte. Which would make her something of a heroine. At least to the British. I'll own I'd have been distinctly disappointed in her."

"Thank you, dearest," Désirée said.

Percy stared from her to Tony as though they were speaking a foreign language.

Tony looked from Sylvie to Percy. "You can leave."

"What?" Percy said.

"You don't have more questions?" Sylvie said.

"Not to discuss with either of you. Not now."

Sylvie looked as though she might protest, then inclined her head. When Percy hesitated, she grabbed his hand and pulled him from the room.

"Make sure Sylvie isn't listening at the door," Tony said.

"Already on it." Julien was halfway across the room.

Désirée stared at Tony, but didn't speak until Julien cracked the door and nodded. "You kept them?" she asked.

"They were from you," Tony said, as though no other answer was necessary.

"Tony. What spy keeps coded letters from another spy?"

"A spy who's in love."

"That could apply to almost everyone in this room. I'm sure none of them were so foolish." Her gaze swept the company.

"I was," Julien said, now leaning against the door. "I kept a letter of Kitty's when I left Buenos Aires."

Kitty stared at him.

"I wasn't sure when I'd see you again."

"I'd probably have been that foolish," Malcolm said. "But Mel wasn't sending the really interesting coded messages to me."

"I didn't," Kitty said. She held out a hand to Julien. "But it doesn't mean I was any less in love, dearest."

"For that matter, I was—" Désirée bit back the words, then gave a rueful smile and shrugged. "No harm in saying it now. I was in love. With you. But it never occurred to me not to burn your letters. Not unless—"

"You thought you could use them?"

"I saved one page that only had a fragment of Lovelace on it. What were you thinking, Tony?"

"They were coded. And hidden with a treasure that had stayed hidden for hundreds of years. That as far as I knew, only I had discovered."

"How bad are they?" Raoul asked.

Désirée frowned and met Tony's gaze. "Descriptions of missions. Most are in the past. Most of the people involved are dead or safe now."

"And accusations," Tony said. "Some concerned times we outwitted each other. Well, mostly times you outwitted me."

"There are still people who could be hurt," Désirée said. "People who are living comfortable lives now. People who were never known to be agents."

"I'm sorry," Tony said.

"If they're my friends, I'm the one who put the words to paper. Some are your friends. And there are things that could embarrass you."

"Embarrassing me is hardly an issue now. I don't care what anyone thinks of me, and no one's going to charge me with treason. It would be too embarrassing for the government."

"It could impact what you can do in future."

"I don't want to do anything that could be impacted in that way."

"So you say now." Désirée moved to his side and touched his face.

"The important thing is that people could be exposed. We need to get the papers back."

Julien crossed his legs at the ankle, still leaning against the wall. "I've been trying to work out who took them if Sylvie didn't."

"Rosalind comes to mind," Tony said.

"Would she have known where they were?" Désirée asked.

"I'm still not sure how anyone knew where they were."

"Percy Rawdon found the treasure," Mélanie pointed out.

"A good point," Tony said. "That rather argues that anyone could. I'm well served for my arrogance."

"In fairness, the panel was left ajar by whoever found it first," Mélanie added.

"When did you last see them?" Malcolm asked.

"The last time I added to the collection," Tony said. "Which was months ago. Before we started planning for Désirée and Sophie to come to Britain. At that point I started burning everything. The risks were higher and I knew they'd be here in person soon."

"Thank goodness for some sense," Désirée said with a smile.

"Sylvie said something about her cousin being exposed," Malcolm said.

Désirée's face went still. "Yes. I didn't know he was her cousin at the time. One of Tony's and my many challenges."

"Désirée—" Tony said.

"They're our friends, Tony. They need to know if they're going to help us. That's why you asked them to stay." She folded her hands and looked round the room. The emerald ring Tony had given her glittered on her fingers. Her face was composed—Désirée Clairineau rarely betrayed any uncertainty—but Mélanie could glimpse in the tension in her hands that it cost her more than her steady gaze let on. "Tony had lists of Royalist agents. I realized I could access them, after Waterloo. When I was in Normandy. When he was visiting Sophie and me in my—our—cottage. I had the chance to take them. I knew friends who were in danger could use them to protect themselves from the Ultra Royalists and avoid arrest. I was living safely in Normandy. I saw a chance to help my comrades. I took the papers from Tony. Which I had done more than once in the past. And he'd done to me. But that was before our relationship had changed."

"We'd made no promises," Tony said quietly.

Désirée shot a glance at him. "That isn't precisely how you put it five years ago."

"I'll own to having been angry in the moment."

"Spoken like a diplomat, my love." Désirée turned back to the group. "I sent the list to friends. I'm not sure whom it went to then. But some of the Royalist agents on it were killed before they could betray anyone. One of them was Sylvie's cousin. I can't say I meant him to be killed. But I admit that if I hadn't taken the list, he wouldn't have been. At least not then."

"He was an agent," Tony said. "He knew what he was risking."

"It's different when it's family," Désirée said.

"One might question if Sylvie knows the meaning of family," Julien said. "But she certainly knows the meaning of revenge. And this is an excuse for it."

"She doesn't have the papers," Raoul said. "And we need to learn who does. We can look for evidence outside when it's daylight."

"Question the staff," Malcolm said. "See if anyone saw anything."

"Thank you," Tony said. "I had hoped it was in the past."

"It's never in the past, my love," Désirée said.

CHAPTER 17

August 1816
Normandy

Tony stared across the cottage sitting room at Désirée. "We were supposed to be past this."

"We're never going to be past it." Désirée set down the coffee tray and glanced round the room. The cushions piled on the settee, the vase of roses on the table, the vines and rose bushes visible through the windows. "Or did you think because we're literally living in a rose-strewn cottage we were less likely to betray each other than we would in a palace?"

"We made a decision." His gaze pinned her to the oak-paneled walls. "To be together."

"We didn't make any promises." She adjusted a cup on the tray. "Our relationship has never been built on promises."

He closed the distance between them in two strides. "We have a child."

She cast an instinctive glance towards the staircase. Sophie was napping upstairs. "I don't believe I've betrayed Sophie."

He took a step back. "You're right. I shouldn't be assuming things."

"You're still a romantic, Tony." She couldn't keep the affectionate mockery from her voice. Or the edge. Because she knew the knife's point they were dancing on.

"Our priorities changed. My priorities changed."

"You're still a British agent."

"And you're not a French agent?"

"The country I had to fight for is gone. I have to find different ways to fight. That doesn't mean we're allies." She folded her arms. "I understand"—her words scraped unexpectedly against her throat— "if you can't accept this."

"Oh no." Tony put a hand on the paneling beside her and leant in. "You're not doing that."

"What?"

"Pushing me away. You've tried that enough in the past."

"I don't think I've ever done anything of the sort. I've pointed out the challenges of the life we're living. I've pointed out that you can't trust me."

"And that isn't pushing me away?"

"Depends on how you feel about trust."

"I trust you."

"My love." She put out a hand and touched his face. "We just made it clear you couldn't."

"I trust Désirée the person. Not the agent."

"If you can disentangle the two, you can see more clearly than I can."

"Isn't that what a lover should do?" His gaze smiled into her own.

She turned her head to the side. "Don't, Tony. Don't try to paper this over."

"I thought you were upset that I was making a point of it in the first place."

"Yes, but if you insist in covering everything in a romantic wash, we'll never be able to really see each other."

He put up a hand and turned her face back to his own. "Désirée, my sweet. I've seen you for a very long time. And you've seen me. Admit it or not. Or we wouldn't be here."

"And where are we?"

"Together. With our child asleep upstairs."

"In hiding. We can't always ignore the outside world."

He dropped his hand to her shoulder. "We can damn well try."

"We can't ignore that we're going to have divided loyalties. We were going to face something like this at some point."

"You took papers from me."

"While you were asleep in our bed. I admit it. Papers that could save friends of mine. We've both always been fair game. We never said we weren't, when we agreed to be domestic."

"No. I made assumptions."

She hesitated. It had to be said. It would have had to be said at some point, sooner or later. She knew that. But that didn't make it any easier. "As I said, if you can't accept it—"

"No." He took her face between his hands. "I made a commitment. To you. I accept who you are. And we're damned well going to make this work."

"You make that sound like a challenge."

He leant in to kiss her. "I know perfectly well you can never resist a challenge."

CHAPTER 18

June 1821
Sawden Park, Surrey

*M*élanie sat up in bed, arms linked round her seafoam silk slip. "Désirée's right."

"About what?" Malcolm perched on the edge of the bed beside her. Neither of them could sleep, but the gray light seeping through the windows still didn't show enough brightness for investigation.

"That it's never in the past."

"No." Malcolm's voice was steady. "We've learnt that. We have to find a way to go on with it. They do as well."

She cast a glance at him. "You're so sensible, darling."

He grinned and reached out to touch her cheek. "Not a lot of other options. But we've managed rather well in recent years, I think."

She tilted her cheek against his hand. "It's someone in the house. Which means if it's not one of us"—meaning their circle of friends, no definition required—"it's someone in the Southcott family. Or one of the staff."

"Yes." Malcolm frowned at the pastoral landscape on the wall opposite. "Could there be anything about you in these letters?"

"You think Tony and Désirée were writing about me?"

The candlelight bounced off Malcolm's steady gaze. "I think you helped Raoul when he and Tony and Stroheim were rescuing Barton and St. Georges from the Conciergerie."

Her fingers tightened round her knees. The silk of her slip was as slippery as promises between spies. "Raoul wanted to keep me out of it. I wouldn't let him."

"I can see that."

She stared at the silk between her fingers, shimmering in the lamplight like the changeable sea. "Supposedly, Tony didn't know. Even if he'd worked it out, hard to see his writing about me to Désirée. It's more likely there's some mention of Raoul. Given that they both worked with him. But Raoul has a pardon. As do I." Though the prince regent hadn't known just what crimes those blanket pardons covered when Malcolm's aunt Frances persuaded him to issue them.

Malcolm reached out to pet Berowne, who had curled up beside her feet. Berowne rolled onto his back and stretched all four legs. He could take up a ridiculous amount of room for a small cat. "It could still cause problems. Especially if he decides to stand for Parliament."

"Tony and Désirée wouldn't mention him by name." Mélanie shifted against the pillows and glanced round the room. "Perhaps—"

She went still. The gray light now filling the room gleamed against something white on the floor by the door. Something that quite certainly not been there when they returned to their room.

Malcolm had seen it too. They got to their feet of one accord and moved to the door.

Something lay on the polished floorboards, in the gap between the door and the Axminster carpet. A folded paper.

"Do you have an admirer writing to you?" Malcolm asked. "Or another agent?"

Mélanie picked up the paper and opened it. The black writing jumped out at her in the pale light. And made her go cold.

KITTY ROLLED OVER, away from the light seeping through the curtains. She'd sworn she wouldn't be able to go back to sleep when they came upstairs after their middle-of-the-night adventure, but apparently she had. Surely Julien hadn't. She stretched out a hand to reach for him and felt a smooth, cool expanse of sheet. She sat up in bed. No sign of Julien in the room, which was filled with pre-dawn light. Perhaps he'd already gone down to start investigating. She swung her legs to the floor and pulled on her dressing gown.

She was reaching for the glass of water on the night table when she caught sight of something on the floor, beside the door. An odd place for Julien to have left her a message. Perhaps he'd forgot to leave it on the pillow or night table and had slid it under the door after he went out of the room. She crossed to the door and bent to retrieve the note.

But the handwriting that met her gaze was not her husband's.

And the message was anything but reassuring.

LAURA SAT up in bed and looked at her husband, bending to retrieve something on the floor by the door. The children had been playing in the room last night, but it wasn't a toy that Raoul was reaching for. It appeared to be a piece of paper. And Raoul was scanning it as though it were anything but amusing.

"What is it?" she asked.

"A warning, I think. Though I can't say from whom." He crossed back to the bed and held the paper out to her.

Laura studied the black ink on the cream-colored paper. "This could be meant for me as much as you."

"A point. Which hardly reassures me."

She had got used to danger long before they married. She'd known his leaving the field hadn't made it go away. That she herself could be a target. But she hadn't expected it at a country house party. More fool her.

"I know." Raoul touched her hair. "We're with friends."

"They aren't all friends."

"No," he said. "They aren't."

KITTY CAME into the breakfast parlor to find Raoul alone at the table, a cup of coffee at his elbow, gaze fixed on a piece of paper on the tablecloth.

"Eventful night," she said, as he looked up and met her gaze. "How are you?"

"I'm not sure." He was frowning.

Kitty moved to a shield-back chair beside him. "Let me guess. You had a rather disturbing note pushed under your door."

Raoul's fingers froze on the handle of his coffee cup. "You got one as well?"

Kitty fished the paper out of the puffed sleeve of the muslin morning gown she'd hastily donned and held it out. She already knew the words by heart.

"You're a fool to try to pretend you aren't what you are."

Raoul set the cup down and held out his own note.

"What do you think you're doing? You can't hide from your past."

"A similar point of view," Kitty said. "Though not one I expected either of us to encounter here."

"No." Raoul reached for the silver coffee pot and poured her a cup. "It's difficult to tell that hand with block capitals, but I'd hazard a guess the same person penned both notes."

"Yes." Kitty took a drink of coffee. "It could be intended for me or for Julien. We certainly both could be said to be pretending. By the way, you haven't seen him this morning, have you?"

Raoul shook his head. "I came down to the breakfast parlor a few minutes ago while Laura checked on the children."

Kitty nodded and took a sip of coffee, keeping her fingers steady on the handle. "He must have started investigating last night's theft. Presumably before the letter was slipped under our door. Perhaps—"

She went still as the breakfast parlor door opened. Tony and Désirée came into the room. They were smiling, but Kitty caught the tension about their mouths and the quick gazes they cast round the breakfast parlor.

"Let me guess," Raoul said. "A note?"

Désirée released her breath. "I was afraid of this. You both got one?"

Kitty and Raoul held out their notes. Désirée and Tony scanned them, then Tony pulled one from his pocket.

"You'll pay for your crimes eventually."

"That's the most threatening," Kitty said. "Though in the same vein."

"How well do you know your staff?" Raoul asked.

"Many of them grew up on the estate," Tony said. "Though I confess I've left the staffing at the various houses to John and—" He hesitated.

"Hetty," Désirée said. "No reason to mention her. She took excellent care of everything for years. You always said so."

"So I did." Tony gave her a quick smile. Then his brows drew together. "I don't like to suspect staff. But I don't think we can escape wondering. The alternative is—one of the family. Or our friends."

The door opened again, this time to admit Malcolm and Mélanie. Kitty saw Raoul go still at their expressions. "You too?" she asked.

They both met her gaze for a moment. "If you mean a mysterious note—" Mélanie pulled a paper from her sleeve and held it out.

"How could you turn your back on everything?"

"It's odd," Kitty said, as they all spread their notes out on the table amid the plates of toast and marmalade and egg cups and cups of coffee. "We're connected but we can't precisely be said to all be on the same side. At least, not in the past. So who would be targeting all of us?"

"Mel and I got threatening notes in Paris once," Malcolm said. "It turned out to be one of our footmen. Who had a legitimate point to make when it came to me."

"We've wondered about the staff," Tony said. "We'll investigate. Because otherwise—"

"It's someone staying here," Raoul said. "Or someone who broke in. I'm not sure which is more alarming. Though one of the guests would certainly be a surprise. Not that we aren't all used to surprises from those in our circle."

"It's also hard to connect it to the missing papers," Mélanie said. "At least, not directly."

"The person who took the papers might have told me I'd pay for my crimes," Désirée said. "But it's difficult to see a connection to the letters to the rest of you."

Malcolm glanced at their note. "I wonder which of us is supposed to have turned our back on everything?"

"I'm the former spy," Mélanie said.

"Well, so am I, for that matter. If not quite on your level. Also a former diplomat."

"And someone could be telling me I'd pay for my crimes as much as Désirée," Tony said. "It's all a matter of perspective." He looked at his guests. "I'm sorry. To have put you in this situation."

"My dear fellow," Raoul said. "If we have enemies, they're going to find us wherever we are. Easier for us all to confront this together."

"As soon as all the staff are up, we can start making discreet inquiries," Malcolm said. "To start with, it would help to have a list of the staff and how long they've been with you."

Tony's face tensed for a moment, but then he nodded.

"THE PANEL WAS ajar when Julien and I came into the library," Kitty said, leading Malcolm into the library. Raoul had gone to investigate outside with Tony and Désirée, and Mélanie was briefing Harry and Cordy and Laura. Kitty had offered to show Malcolm the passage. She hadn't, Malcolm noted, suggested getting Julien.

"We should light a lamp." Malcolm stopped beside a table with a lamp and dug a flint from his pocket.

"Whoever took the papers must have come back through the library, or gone out the end of the passage by the folly well before Percy," Kitty said. "Odd none of us heard them."

"That could argue one of the staff. Or one of the guests whose bedchamber was closer to the stairs than yours and Julien's or mine and Mel's." Malcolm struck the flint. The lamp flared to life.

"Yes, I thought of that. Which makes Rosalind less likely. She'd have had to walk right past our room. Malcolm—" Kitty hesitated as Malcolm adjusted the flame of the lamp. "Have you seen Julien this morning?"

"No. Mel and I came right to the breakfast parlor. He wasn't—"

"In our bed?" Kitty gave a faint smile, though there was a line between her brows. "He was when we went back to bed after chasing Sylvie. But not when I woke up. And, yes, I used to be able to tell when someone slipped out of my bed in the night. Marriage is apparently making me soft."

Her eyes belied the irony in her voice. Malcolm touched her arm. "If he didn't leave a note, he must expect to be back soon."

"Or there wasn't time. Julien and I both know there isn't always time for reassurance. He must have gone out early, before the secret note was delivered. I can't see Julien ignoring or simply leaving it. I'm sure he'll turn up before long." But Malcolm caught the edge beneath Kitty's voice. This went against the man Julien had become lately. And though one never knew what went on inside another's marriage, Malcolm suspected it went against the unspoken contract of his marriage with Kitty.

"Perhaps he's discovered a new secret passage or hiding place. We'll see if we can find him." Malcolm squeezed her shoulders. "I may not be a match for Julien, but you certainly are."

Kitty shook her head. "Ten to one he's somewhere perfectly obvious and he'll laugh at me for worrying. Do me a favor and don't let him know how foolish I've been."

"Word of honor. Though I can't imagine Julien laughing at you." Malcolm grinned and picked up the lamp. "Let's see if we can find who took the papers before Julien shows his face."

CHAPTER 19

*F*rederica stared at Cordelia. "Percy stole the Southcott jewels?"

"He had them in his coat last night."

"Percy managed to *find* the Southcott jewels?"

"Apparently someone else managed to find them first and left the hiding place ajar. It was a compartment in the secret passage."

"That makes a bit more sense. Though it's still very enterprising of Percy." Frederica shook her head. "The fact that he found them shocks me more than that he was willing to steal them. That should be surprising. But it isn't." She folded her arms and hugged her elbows. "It's an odd thing. Thinking your parents have found something much sweeter and simpler than your own circumstances and hoping they can make it work."

"My mother's happy with my stepfather," Cordelia said. "Happier than she was with my father, I think. I noticed that from the first, though I confess I never wanted to dwell on their romance."

"One doesn't, with parents. But I'm old enough now to appreciate it. And to keenly hope my children follow their example instead of Percy's and mine." Frederica frowned across the lawn at the line of birch. She and Cordelia had gone out onto the terrace to talk. "It's odd. They seemed to want us to be happy. And I truly believe they did. But I can't say they emphasized love. Well, in the sort of general way everyone talks about it every season. When parents talk about finding a suitable attachment and a gentleman assures one of the violence of his feelings after discussing the dowry with one's father over port. Not the sort of love one runs risks for. Loving a spy for the opposite side. Loving a steward. Overturning a marriage. Not that I'd advocate that—"

"Really?" Cordelia said.

"Well, not in the general run of things." Frederica's frown deepened. "I can't really imagine going to those extremes. Even given that Percy—well, no sense wrapping plain facts up in clean linen. It's rather difficult to imagine a marriage being more of a disaster than ours is. That is—" She bit back her words.

"Oh, don't worry," Cordelia said. "Mine wasn't really a disaster in that sense. Even before I made such a mull of things with George. But if I'd married George, my marriage would have been even more of a disaster."

"And Mama's and Papa's wasn't," Frederica said. "I mean, I'm quite sure they still like each other. Which is more than can be said for Percy and me. It's not contempt or even dislike that's driving them. It's that they love other people." She paused, arms folded over her chest. "I can't imagine loving like that. I'm rather stunned. Truth be told, I'm rather envious."

"You're a generation younger than your parents. You have a lot of time."

"Cordy. Are you advocating scandal?"

"Not for its own sake. But I wouldn't shy away from happiness for fear of scandal. And happiness can take different forms. I never thought to find what I did."

Frederica nodded. "I've known Wilcox forever. I've always liked him. But do you trust her?"

"Who?" Cordelia asked, though it was blindingly obvious.

"Désirée Clairineau. She's charming. I find myself liking her.

And I forget everything else. And then I can't help but think about all the other people she must have charmed through the years. Charmed and betrayed. Including Papa."

"It doesn't seem to have done lasting damage."

"Meaning he's still bewitched."

"Meaning your father seems to see her quite clearly, from what I can tell."

"How can anyone ever know that about anyone else? He may trust her now, but can one ever really know another person?"

"Well, no, I suppose not. That's one of the first rules of historical investigation, actually. One has to trust one's getting the closest approximation possible."

"Is that what you do with Harry?"

"I suppose—well, yes. I mean, at the start he was a total cipher. I couldn't imagine why he wanted to marry me. Even that first year we were married I scarcely got to know him better. No, that's not quite true. I was starting to see him in bits and pieces. He really came into focus for me before Waterloo. And then after. For a bit after we reconciled, I was terrified it would go wrong. I'm not now. And now I'd say I know him as well as anyone."

Freddy looked sideways at her. "I've seen you. You can exchange a glance and know what the other is thinking."

"Yes. But still—I can't claim to know everything. He's still his own person. Just as I am. It would be rather dreadful if marriage, even a happy marriage, took that away."

"So Papa can't really know Désirée."

"From what I've seen, I think he may know her as well as anyone ever knows another person. Like Harry and me, they've been through a lot. More than we have, actually."

"But you never betr—" Frederica bit her words back.

"Betrayed Harry? I betrayed him in the worst way possible. In a way that I suspect hurt more than anything Désirée did to your father. Or that he did to her. And they were honest about their differences. That matters a lot."

Frederica cast a glance towards the house where Désirée was now mistress. "It must be appalling to be bested."

"But it might make one admire the other person. A good musician appreciates another musician and doesn't feel outdone."

"Yes, but one musician isn't taking anything from the other."

"Well, they might be taking a job or a commission, but I do see your point."

Freddie's fair brows knotted over her blue eyes. "You said there were papers with the jewels. Papers of Désirée's."

"Letters she wrote to your father, apparently. Drafts of letters he wrote to her too, I think."

"And someone took these before Percy found the jewels."

"So it seems. Unless Percy is playing a very deep game. Found the treasure on his own and made it look like someone else had found it first."

"Ha."

"Did you hear anything last night?"

"Cordy." Frederica turned from the window to face Cordelia. "Percy and I haven't shared a bedchamber for any part of the night for almost a decade."

"I didn't necessarily mean Percy. Someone else was moving about last night and took the papers."

"You mean someone at the house party."

"Or one of the staff. Unless someone broke into the house, which is not impossible, though it seems more surprising."

Frederica frowned. "I can't imagine—though in truth, it's hard to imagine any of the things that have happened recently." Her fingers tightened on her arms. "I did wake at one point in the night. I'm not sure when. It was still quite dark out. I rolled over and realized a sound had woken me. Footsteps in the passage. I assumed—well, when people are moving about at night at a house party, the assumption is fairly obvious."

"Could you tell anything about the person?"

"Well, no, obviously I didn't see—"

"I mean were the footsteps light or heavy? Did they seem to be wearing shoes?"

Frederica's eyes widened. "You're good at this, Cordy. I didn't realize—"

"Well, I have learnt a bit in the past few years. This is hardly my first investigation."

"No. I didn't think—" Frederica glanced across the lawn as though conjuring memories. "I don't think the person was wearing shoes. The footsteps weren't particularly heavy but they weren't light either, if that makes sense. They were quick. Somehow, I think it was a man. But I could be wrong."

"Do you have any idea what time it was?"

"Yes, actually. I didn't get back to sleep right away and I heard the long-case clock by the stairs. So it was just before two-fifteen."

That was early for it to have been Sylvie, according to the timeline Mélanie had given her. Though it might have been Percy who had gone out and come back in and gone out again. Still, anything that helped them establish a timeline was good.

"We should share this with the others," Cordelia said. "If you don't mind."

"No. Anything to help. Especially given the trouble Percy's caused."

Of one accord, Cordelia and Freddie turned and moved to the salon. And nearly collided with St. Ives, coming through the French windows.

"Oh, there you all are." St. Ives strode onto the terrace, seemingly unaware he'd nearly bumped into the two of them. "Has either of you seen Sylvie?"

"We breakfasted quite early," Cordelia said. "I haven't seen a number of the party."

"Sylvie usually has chocolate in her room," Frederica said.

"Yes, but she's usually up by now. Helena hasn't seen her either. Or Rosy. Not that they spend time together in the general run of things. But damn it, someone must have seen her."

"It's a very large house, St. Ives," Frederica said. "Lots of places for a person to get lost."

"Perhaps she's with the children," Cordelia suggested. "There's a lottery tickets game in progress in the drawing room."

St. Ives frowned. "You don't know my wife very well, Lady Cordelia."

"I've known Sylvie for years," Cordelia said. "She may not spend as much time with her children as some of us do, but she doesn't entirely ignore them."

St. Ives gave something suspiciously close to a snort. "I may not be as clever as some of you. But this is damned odd."

Freddie reached for the handle of the French window, which her brother hadn't closed behind him. "It's hardly the only thing odd at this house party, St. Ives. Or in this family."

CHAPTER 20

July 1811
Sawden Park, Surrey

ony sprang over the lawn and knocked the intruder to the ground, then drew back and looked down into her face in the moonlight. "What are you doing here? I could have killed you."

"You don't kill people, Tony." Désirée sat up and pushed her brown hair out of her face. It was falling free of its pins. "At least, not unless they're seriously trying to kill you first." She braced herself on her hands and leant back to look at him. "I needed to see you."

"You're in England."

"Yes, I had noticed that. It's not the first time. Don't ask questions. I came to give you a warning. I don't trust even the best couriers and codes."

He scanned her face. He knew full well how adept she was at lying, though he'd swear he could read the urgency in her gaze. "What?"

"Can we go into that little stone building? Which looks as

though someone in the last fifty years spent a lot of money trying to make into an approximation of a medieval ruin."

"Sixty-five, actually." He held out a hand and helped her to her feet. "My favorite spot to escape with a book."

She took his hand and let him pull her up, then glanced round the rolling, moon-drenched lawns. "How do you manage not to go mad in the country?"

"I quite like the solitude. A chance to think. And a chance to not be anyone but myself. How did you know I was here?"

"You don't have a great deal of faith in my sources. Besides, you told me this was your favorite house."

"It is. The place I feel most at home. Next to—"

"A mission?"

"Anywhere you are."

"Tony, that's charming. And not helpful."

He kept hold of her hand as they walked to the folly. "I didn't say it to be helpful. I said it because it's true."

"I'm a weakness. I've warned you that often enough."

"Well. I've always been addicted to risk. Besides, something brought you here. Unless you're trying to kill me again?"

"Not this time." Désirée climbed the steps of the folly and dropped down on a stone bench. "How much do you know about your daughter-in-law?"

"Sylvie?" Tony ducked beneath the archway and followed her. "My son is besotted with her and she is most definitely not besotted with him. I thought having her would make him happy. Or at least that having a different wife from her would make him unhappy. But it can be hard to have the object of one's desire constantly out of reach." He leant against the stone wall by one of the arched windows, legs crossed at the ankle.

"So it can. Sylvie is also an agent for Carfax. Hubert Mallinson."

"Ah." Tony folded his arms. "I suspected as much."

"Is she working for you too?"

"Hardly. You know Hubert and I don't always see eye to eye. To put it mildly. In fact, I don't think he trusts me. He suspects I have a French mistress."

"You'll have to introduce me to her sometime."

"Next time there's a mirror about."

Désirée's gaze glittered in the shadows. "How much do you know about Sylvie?"

"I'm quite sure she's gone through my papers a few times. It's all right. I'm careful with what I leave about. Surely you didn't come all this way to warn me about Sylvie working for Hubert."

"No." Désirée leant back against the wall. "To tell you she's also working for Fouché."

Tony went still. "That is interesting. You're sure?"

"One of my agents intercepted a communication between them. She has a cousin working for him as well. I could show you—"

"That's not necessary." Tony shifted his shoulders. The stones suddenly seemed to jab him in the back. "I suppose she wants a foot in both camps. Depending on how things go. Her family lost everything in the Terror. I imagine she'd like to get it back, one way or another." He watched Désirée for a moment. "Are you worried she's told Fouché something about us?"

"Could she have?"

"I very much doubt it. Nothing from you, even coded, is anywhere she could have seen. You needn't worry."

"I didn't come here because I was worried about myself." Désirée unfolded herself from the bench. "This is serious, Tony. You're facing all sorts of exposure."

"I appreciate the warning. But I've taken rather good care of myself for the past two decades."

"It's still a grand adventure to you." Désirée moved to stand in front of him and put her hands on his chest. The moonlight spilling through the windows slanted across her face and lit her eyes. "And you think everyone plays by the same gentlemen's rules as you. But not everyone is playing that game. Sylvie's out to win. And she's ruthless. Possibly as much as I am."

He smiled and brushed his fingers against her cheek. "I've handled you."

"She's also not in love with you."

"Good god, I hope not." He stilled, his fingers in the vicinity of her ear. "Wait a minute, what did you just say?"

"It slipped out." She leant closer. She wasn't wearing perfume, but he could smell the scent of her hair. "Don't be foolish, Tony. Watch your back. She's trying to claw her way back to what she thinks she's lost. That's not me, but I understand that sort of desperation. In a way I don't think you ever could."

He leant in and kissed her. "What exactly do you know?"

"Fouché's made overtures to Hubert Mallinson. Or Hubert's made overtures to him, I'm not quite sure which. And Sylvie's carried information between them."

"Christ."

"I don't think she'll go so far towards Fouché she jeopardizes her relationship with Hubert. Or rather, her position. But she's willing to go quite far."

Tony frowned. "Poor St. Ives. He was wise enough to love a brilliant and capable woman. But I don't think he has the least idea of the extent of her capabilities. Hetty wanted him to marry one of her friends' daughters. I thought he should be free to choose. Not the first time Hetty and I've disagreed. I still maintain everyone should be able to choose their marriage partner. But I'll confess there are times I've wondered if St. Ives wouldn't be happier if he'd followed the path his mother wanted. And though Hetty wouldn't dream of saying anything, I'm quite sure at times she blames me for our son's unhappiness."

"You don't know that he would be happier. And surely the duchess's friend's daughter deserved to be able to make her own choice as well."

"A point." Tony stared at the stones of the wall opposite. Seemingly worn smooth by centuries, yet only a couple of decades older than he was himself.

"You worry about him," Désirée said.

"Of course. He's my child. I worry about all my children."

"Do you worry about the girls as much?"

"Rosalind's still a child. Freddie and Helena are—"

"Settled? You've told me what you think of Frederica's husband."

Tony passed a hand over his face. "Fair enough. I do worry about Freddie. Perhaps I credit her with more sense to handle her situation than St. Ives. Or perhaps it's that he's—"

"Your heir."

Tony looked down into her eyes. He'd swear they could cut him open and see straight through to his soul. "He is. No sense in denying it. Disapprove inherited privilege all you will. To own the truth, I'm not sure what I think of it anymore. But it's a legacy that's been passed on to me and that I'll pass on to him. For the moment—for the foreseeable future—I'm the steward of the Southcott legacy. And I wouldn't be a very good steward if I didn't worry about what St. Ives made of it."

"I know." She pushed his hair off his forehead. Her fingers lingered against his temple. "It's part of what makes you you. I know you worry about him. Perhaps he's more like you than you realize."

"Are you saying you're like Sylvie?"

"I hope not. Though we share certain characteristics. And I'd say anyone who gets too close to either of us would do well to beware."

"From what I've seen of my daughter-in-law, I can't see her going into enemy terrain to warn anyone."

"People can surprise you. At times I surprise myself." She cast a glance round the shadowy stones and the moonlit lawn outside the windows. "I've told you what I came to say. Risky to stay longer."

He laced his fingers through her own. "You've come this far. Stay."

"In your house? Have you gone mad?"

"You're the one who came here."

"To give you a warning. That you don't seem to be taking to heart."

"I'm inestimably grateful for it. But I don't see how your staying the night makes things worse."

"If it gets out—"

"My staff are very discreet. And if the news gets out that I had a woman here, I can't see how Sylvie can use it."

"Because you've had so many women here?"

"No comment. That is—" He touched her cheek. "The rules of my marriage had changed before I met you. But I'd never say I was a great one for dalliance. And as it happens, I've never brought anyone else here."

"All the more reason for us not to rouse suspicions."

"Désirée." He set his hands on her shoulders. "Are you saying the two of us can't outwit anyone when we put our minds to it?"

"Ah." She tilted her head back. "You know just how to get my attention."

"That was the general idea."

She laughed and pulled his head down to her own. He pulled her closer against him and slid his fingers into her hair. She laced her fingers through his own. They could hold hands as they ran across the lawn. If he could bring himself to let go long enough—

A pistol shot whistled overhead.

CHAPTER 21

June 1821
Sawden Park, Surrey

Mélanie came out of the drawing room from checking on the children's game of lottery tickets (which the St. Ives and Rawdon teenagers had well in hand) to greet Harry as he came through the green baize door from the servants' stairs. His gaze was focused, which wasn't unusual in an investigation, but his brows were drawn with unaccustomed concern.

"What is it?" she asked.

"I was talking with the servants. One of the footmen is missing. Alfred Higgins. Hasn't been seen since last night."

"Suggestive," Mélanie said.

"Yes, I thought so. Apparently, Higgins was hired about three months ago when the housekeeper got word Tony was taking up residence and thought they needed more staff. No one knows much about him."

Which meant there might be an agent who had got himself hired into the household and was now on the run with Tony and

Désirée's letters. Reason enough for the lingering worry in Harry's gaze. And yet—"What else?" she asked.

"One of the housemaids mentioned that Lady St. Ives wasn't in her room when she took up her chocolate this morning."

"Given everything going on, Sylvie could have had a number of reasons to rise early."

"So she could." Harry's voice was even. "But no one's seen her since. St. Ives has been asking questions. He practically accosted Cordy and Frederica a bit ago."

Mélanie cast a glance round the hall. But there was no need for secrets from Harry. "Julien's been missing from early this morning. Kitty asked Malcolm after breakfast. You haven't seen him?"

Harry shook his head. "Not on my end. Of course, all sorts of data can correlate without meaning anything."

Mélanie touched his arm. "Spoken like a scholar. But sometimes one can't ignore inferences."

RAOUL KNELT DOWN by the panel at the end of the passage that opened onto the folly. "Can you lift the lantern?"

Laura held the lantern higher. "You look happy."

He cast a grin at her over his shoulder that flashed white in the shadows. "I wouldn't claim to be unhappy, but this is a challenging situation."

"And you thrive on challenge. You're back at work. You have a mission."

"I'm glad if we can help. And don't pretend you don't enjoy the challenge."

Laura returned her husband's grin. "By no means." In fact, she knew it all too well. The delight of a role to play in a mission when she'd been spending time writing, teaching the children, devising curricula. All of which she enjoyed. But which didn't quicken her blood in quite the same way. And she at least found a satisfaction in writing and teaching that she wasn't sure Raoul did in anything outside the spy game. She hadn't seen quite this light in his eyes since he'd been wounded.

He peered at the stone wall in the light of the lamp and then scraped against it with a needle. He held the needle up to the lantern light.

Traces of thread. Dark blue. And faint traces of silver that shimmered in the lantern light.

"Interesting," he said.

Laura bent closer and pictured the guests round the dinner table the night before. She met her husband's gaze. "This complicates things."

"So it does."

"Are you disappointed?"

Raoul got to his feet. "Not precisely. But I'm weighing how to play the scene that has to come next."

CHAPTER 22

July 1811
Sawden Park, Surrey

ésirée and Tony slammed each other to the stone floor as the shot pinged overhead. Tony lifted his head, which was pressed between her shoulder and her ear. "This happens to us far too often."

"Given the lives we lead, it's surprising it doesn't happen more."

"A point. I never did hear who Jacques was working for when he tried to kill you the night we met."

"Fouché. I think."

"Interesting." Tony pushed himself up on his knees and scanned the moon-drenched lawn through the windows. "Do you think you were followed here?"

"I'm not easy to follow. But one can never be sure." She scrambled out from underneath him and pushed herself to her knees. Her fingers touched damp on the stone and came away red. "You're wounded."

"Flesh wound."

Another shot rang out overhead. Even if the shooter was a rifleman, they had twenty seconds. Tony grabbed her hand, tugged her to the stone wall, and pressed his fingers against a stone outcropping. A panel slid open. He pulled her inside.

"Sometimes I have cause to be grateful to my ancestors." Tony kicked the panel closed.

They were in a dark passage. Slits let in minimal light—enough to see close stone walls. Tony started forwards, but Désirée gripped his arm and tugged at his cravat. Fortunately, she had considerable experience removing it. She unwound it, then bound it round his arm, more by feel than sight. It would stop the bleeding until she could bandage it properly.

"I'm not going to collapse," he said.

"No sense not being careful."

"From you that's highly amusing."

"I don't take unnecessary risks."

He took her hand and they made their way along the passage. It slanted down, and from the change in the air—damp and close—and the lack of light, she assumed they were underground. The passage slanted up again and ended in a short flight of steps. She sensed more than saw the solid wall in front of them. Then Tony pressed a spot on the wall and another panel slid back.

Moonlight, unexpectedly bright after the darkness, glinted off the gilded spines of books, the glass fronts of bookcases, ormolu on bits of furniture. She should have known Tony would have a superb library.

She glanced round the shadows. "Rather like your safe cottage. Only grander."

Tony struck a flint to a lamp and took her hand again. "The servants are abed. I don't keep a large staff when it's just me, and I don't like to make them stay up."

"Good of you."

His eyes glinted down at her. "Touché."

They went into a high-ceilinged marble-tiled hall and up a

heavy wooden staircase that smelt of lemon oil. The lamp light slid over portraits of people in clothes of bygone eras with a vague resemblance to Tony. A landing and a passage.

He opened a door and drew her inside. Stillness. More bookshelves, a chest of drawers. The mass of a four-poster. They were in his bedchamber. For the first time. That made it different, somehow. For reasons she couldn't explain.

"What about your valet?" she murmured.

"He's visiting his parents."

"Good god."

"Surely you aren't surprised my valet has parents."

"No, that you know he does."

"We grew up together. His father was an underbutler at Chevenings. Another of our estates. When we were boys, we played tag and went fishing together. You really need to get past some of your prejudices, my sweet." He set the lamp down, moved to the windows, and drew the curtains. "Just to be safe."

"Where's your medical supply box?"

"You've already bandaged me."

"I want to make sure it isn't infected."

Tony was too sensible to argue. He produced a medical supply box from the chest of drawers, and a bottle of cognac that stood on top. She unwound the cravat and splashed brandy on lint to clean the wound. "Assuming I wasn't followed, who might want to shoot at you?"

He sucked in his breath but kept his arm steady. "Surely you'd be more likely to know about that than I."

"Not necessarily. Jacques was working for my people."

"A point. Hubert Mallinson has never been very happy with me, but I have a hard time seeing him trying to have me killed. Failure of imagination, perhaps. For that matter, I'm not much of a favorite with Castlereagh either."

"You think the British foreign secretary tried to have you killed?" Désirée knotted off a clean dressing round Tony's arm.

"You think Fouché tried to have you killed."

"Fouché was making overtures to the Royalists then. He was afraid I knew too much."

"Of course, it could be Fouché coming after me. With information supplied by my daughter-in-law."

She held his gaze as she snipped off the ends of the bandage. "Do you think she would?"

"Well, Sylvie would have a number of things to gain from getting rid of me. If she's working for Hubert and Fouché, both have their reasons to want to see me gone. And I think Sylvie would quite like to be Duchess of Bamford."

"I'm sorry. This can't be easy to contemplate."

"Good god. Is this Désirée Clairineau talking?"

"I try not to give way to human emotions. That doesn't mean I'm deaf to them."

Tony tugged his shirtsleeve down over his bandaged arm. "I flatter myself I've always been reasonably clear-eyed when it comes to Sylvie. Though I'll own it's not a pleasant thing to hear about someone one has sat down to dinner with."

"Oh, when it comes to the people spies sit down to dinner with…"

Tony grinned, then picked up the cognac decanter again and poured two glasses.

She accepted the cognac, touched her glass to his, and perched on the edge of the bed. He took a drink, then knelt down without speaking and pulled her boots off with his good hand.

"You always know just what a woman needs."

"You must have been traveling a long time."

"I confess this bed looks very comfortable."

"You can just go to sleep."

She flopped back against the pillows and tugged him down next to her. "That would be a sad waste."

He grinned as he settled into the pillows beside her.

"It's a comfortable room, Tony." She looked from the green

velvet canopy to the Renaissance oils on the walls. "It looks like you. And of course, it's wildly extravagant. Not that I'm not known to be extravagant."

He touched her face. "It's nice. Having you here."

"When I think of the spycraft it ought to have taken to get into your bedchamber."

"Are you telling me the past decade hasn't been elaborate spycraft?"

"Not just spycraft." She pulled him down for a kiss. "You need to rest your arm."

"Oh, don't worry." He smoothed her hair back from her face with his good hand. "You have no notion what I can do one-handed..."

CHAPTER 23

June 1821
Sawden Park, Surrey

Désirée scanned Mélanie Rannoch's face in the late morning sun slanting across the lawn. "Any updates?" Tempting as it was to assist with the inquiries, it made more sense for people less connected to the household than she and Tony to do the questioning. Which left her a bit nowhere in a world that was technically hers and yet in which she remained an alien.

"One of your footmen disappeared this morning," Mélanie said. "An Alfred Higgins."

Désirée frowned. She could picture Alfred Higgins. Average height. Fair hair. Blue eyes. Early to mid-thirties. "He was hired recently. I confess I haven't spoken much with him." She'd made it a point to try to converse with all of the staff, but Alfred Higgins had replied in polite monosyllables. Embarrassment at being spoken to by the duke's mistress, she'd thought. Now—"I don't know where Mrs. Worthing found him, I'm afraid. But I've certainly planted enough agents as servants through the years. I've played the role myself on more than one occasion."

Mélanie nodded. "Harry and Malcolm are talking to Tony about him. Two horses are gone from the stables. But Sylvie also hasn't been seen all day and St. Ives is raising questions. And Julien hasn't been seen either."

Mélanie had an enviably evenhanded way of delivering challenging news. "Interesting. A number of ways they could all be connected. But if Alfred Higgins is an agent and has the papers, our odds of recovering them have gone down significantly. For that matter, if Sylvie was deceiving us last night and has them, the odds are challenging as well. And Tony will never forgive himself." She said it calmly. Because, really, there was no sense in doing otherwise. And it wasn't as though she hadn't been in worse situations.

"It's concerning," Mélanie agreed. "But I strongly suspect Julien has gone after one or both of them. I'm always inclined to bet on Julien over anyone else."

"I'm sorry," Désirée said. "This could unravel and reflect on you. Or Raoul. We're not the safest friends."

Mélanie shook her her head, strands of dark hair stirring about her face. "In that sense, no agents are safe friends. We're used to the risk. And something like this could surface at any point." She hesitated a moment. "You get used to it over time. Living in a ridiculously protected world with unimaginable luxuries. And with risk there, just under the surface. It was worse when Malcolm didn't know the truth. Even then, I'd manage not to think about it for days at a time."

"I remember you in Vienna," Désirée said. "At the sleighing party and the masked ball at the Hofburg and some other occasions. You made an indelible impression."

"Probably because of the black circles under my eyes. By the winter, we'd all been running on a few hours' sleep a night for months."

"You always looked impeccable. You always smiled. But it was the look behind the smile that resonated. What you did was remarkable."

"Attended events and changed my clothes five times a day. The same thing a score of other people did in Vienna."

"Pretended to be someone not yourself."

Mélanie's fingers closed on the sleeves of her rose-colored sarcenet spencer. "Isn't that what you did? Isn't that what we all do?"

"But you did it longer. I saw you in Brussels as well. And you did it with the person you love."

"I started doing it for the mission. And then when I stopped, it seemed the least I owed him."

"Difficult to build a relationship on owing."

"Difficult to build a relationship on spying."

"A good point. I think I sometimes went out of my way to show Tony how ruthless I was because I couldn't bear the thought that my feelings for him might have impacted my work."

"But you didn't change."

"I changed immeasurably. But I don't think I ever tried to be a different person because of him. If I'm still a good judge of people, I think you've found your way back to yourself?"

"I think so. Though I think I'm still discovering who I am. And I think Malcolm understands."

"Does he need to?"

"No. Yes. That's part of being in a relationship, isn't it? Caring about what the other person thinks? Malcom says he doesn't need me to be a political wife."

"But you still are, more than he realizes?"

"There are still things he needs. There are still things I like about it, if I'm honest."

Désirée nodded. "I'm still working that out. But yes. I've found myself worrying about Tony's walking away from his diplomatic work. The same work that had us on opposite sides. I can't imagine being a diplomatic wife. But I suppose there are some things I'd do to help Tony."

"Like hosting a house party for his wife and her lover and their children and spouses?"

Désirée's mouth curved in a smile. "Touché."

"It's an odd world. The rules are appalling. But the people aren't, for the most part. Thoughtless. Arrogant, at times. But when you get to know them on their own terms, many of them are surprisingly agreeable."

"I've seen enough to see that. Though I'm likely to mingle less in this world than I did in the past. Divorced couples aren't part of Mayfair society."

"Raoul and Laura go a surprising number of places. And the Hollands have established a circle all of their own. But that rather depends on what you and Tony want."

Désirée went still. "I confess I hadn't thought—or perhaps I had, to a degree. Without quite acknowledging it. Tony says he's done with all that—the diplomatic corps and the rest of it. But I don't know that I could stand in his way if he wanted to return. Nor can I quite see myself being a diplomatic hostess."

"I'm sure he wouldn't want you to be one, if it wasn't what you wanted."

"No. Tony's always been considerate. But then I wouldn't want to hold him back from doing what he wanted."

"Nor would I with Malcolm."

"So you don't let him see how much you still do?"

Mélanie smiled. "Perhaps."

"That's the worst of the damned papers. That they could cut off options for Tony. In the past, I never had to fear exposure outside of a mission. Now—" Désirée shook her head. "It's an adjustment. Not being on one's own."

"Even after almost eight years of marriage." Mélanie's fingers tightened on her arms. "Ever since Raoul was attacked, I've been afraid of where the next threat would come from. Afraid of letting down my guard. But I didn't foresee this. That's the problem. One never knows." She glanced towards the house. "Let's see what Malcolm and Harry have learnt from Tony. You'll feel better with something to do."

They started for the terrace, but before they'd gone a half-dozen paces, they saw a man approaching round the side of the house. Mélanie went still. Désirée hesitated, taking him in. Slight, wiry, graying hair, sharp-featured face, eyes that might be gray or green or blue or brown behind spectacle lenses. They weren't precisely strangers. She'd encountered him before, more than once. But he hadn't always been using his true name, and she never had. There were two ways to play this. Direct or subterfuge. She'd be inclined to the direct. But she wasn't on her own. She had Tony to consider. And though she wasn't a diplomatic wife, this called for diplomacy.

Mélanie drew in her breath. "Do you—"

"I can handle it," Désirée said. She walked forwards to greet the British spymaster she had tilted against for two decades. "May I help?"

CHAPTER 24

*H*ubert Mallinson met her gaze, his own at once sharp and opaque behind the spectacle lenses, and she was quite sure he remembered their past meetings as well. "Mademoiselle Clairineau, I presume? My apologies for the intrusion. My name is Mallinson. I'm a colleague of Bamford's. And I believe my nephew Julien and his family are staying with you. Along with the Rannochs." He nodded at Mélanie, who had followed Désirée.

"Yes. They're all close friends of ours. Did you come to see Julien and Kitty?"

"In a manner of speaking. I was on my way to our own country house and I had a message to deliver to my nephew. I remembered he was staying here and thought I would take the liberty of intruding on you to deliver it."

It was palpably false and for all his skillful delivery, Désirée was quite sure he knew as much. And also knew she wouldn't call him on it. Not with Tony in the picture. She was getting a taste of life in the beau monde. The life Mélanie had been living for almost a decade.

"Of course. We don't stand on ceremony. As I'm sure is clear from our quite unorthodox living arrangements. Do please come in. May we offer you refreshment? I would take you to your nephew directly, but I'm afraid he isn't here at present."

Hubert Mallinson frowned. "It's not like Julien to go tramping about. And he's never been one for fishing."

"I would never dream of asking my guests for particulars of their activities," Désirée said with the artless smile she'd found very effective in a number of masquerades. "I imagine he'll be back before long."

Hubert Mallinson pushed his spectacles up on his nose. "As bad as that? What sort of mission is he off on?"

Désirée gave an even more artless smile. "If that were the case, surely you can't imagine he'd have shared particulars with me."

"That would rather depend on the mission, I should think. Mélanie?"

"You know Julien," Mélanie said. "It took him months to start entering our house by the door instead of through a window. And he still has a way of melting away at unexpected moments. Oh, here's Kitty."

Whether she had noted Hubert's arrival or it was some lucky accident, Kitty was approaching across the lawn.

"Uncle Hubert." She lifted her cheek for his kiss. "Do you need help or do you want information?"

"Must you assume it's one or the other?"

"With you?" Kitty stepped back in the circle of his arm. "Yes."

"Glad to see you've lost none of your sharpness. Where's Julien?"

Kitty cast a quick glance at Désirée and Mélanie.

"Don't worry, they haven't told me anything," Hubert said.

"He's either with Sylvie or chasing her," Kitty said.

"That's quite an admission."

"Yes, I was trying to work out if it was safe to tell you. But if you have anything to do with it, I probably haven't betrayed anything. And you might betray something to me. And if you don't, it might be helpful for you to know."

"You don't seem very concerned."

"About Julien?" Kitty asked. "Well, he can certainly take care of himself, but of course I'm a bit concerned. About Sylvie being with Julien? No, I'm not. At a certain point one has to trust."

Hubert gave a grunt of acknowledgment. "Anyone who's seen you with Julien wouldn't think you have to worry. But as it happens, Sylvie's the reason I'm here."

"You're looking for her?" Mélanie said.

"She sent for me," Hubert said.

Désirée started and saw Kitty and Mélanie do the same.

"Did she say why?" Kitty asked.

"No. Merely that she had information to share that it would be to my value to receive, and she suggested I stop here on my way to my own property." He looked from Kitty to Mélanie. "Would you happen to have an idea of what she meant to tell me?"

"No," Kitty said with a dazzling smile.

"Not that we'd tell you if we did," Mélanie said.

"I fully suspected that. Of course, I might add that I didn't need to tell you Sylvie sent for me. And I fully realize that admission may make you shift tactics on your own end."

Kitty kept her gaze steady on her husband's uncle. Désirée watched the give and take. To think she had thought the Southcott family dynamics complicated. "So why did you make it?" Kitty asked.

"If you were in my position, would you trust Sylvie?" Hubert said.

"It's difficult to imagine anyone trusting Sylvie St. Ives. It's also difficult imagining anyone trusting you."

"Yes, I thought you might say that. But Sylvie's attitude towards me—"

"Sylvie has positioned herself as more your enemy than she is Julien's. Or than Julien is yours."

"Precisely. Which makes me wonder—"

"If she was trying to lure you into a trap?" Mélanie asked.

"Precisely."

"And yet you came?" Désirée said.

"Would you have been able to avoid being curious?"

"By no means." Kitty folded her arms. "It's possible she meant you to arrive and discover both herself and Julien missing."

Hubert pushed his spectacles up on his nose. His brows drew together over the frame. "Kitty, are you suggesting Sylvie kidnapped Julien?"

"No. Not unless Julien went along with it for reasons of his own."

"Or they planned it together?" Hubert asked.

"I wouldn't rule that out, though I can't quite work out the whys and wherefores."

Hubert's brows snapped together. "Never mind the whys and wherefores. I can't believe this is coincidental."

"Nor can I," Kitty agreed. "I suspect Julien went after Sylvie. Or went with Sylvie to try to co-opt her. The more interesting question is why she'd send for you."

"An interesting question indeed," Hubert said. "Perhaps—"

He broke off as Tony strolled up to join them.

"Hubert." Tony took up a position by Désirée that was definitely protective. She was amused and might have been annoyed if it weren't so adorable. "Are you here to see your nephew and his wife?"

"No, to see your daughter-in-law, as it happens."

Tony frowned.

"I agree," Hubert said. "I'm as surprised as anyone. But apparently she isn't here."

"I imagine she'll turn up before long," Tony said. "Though judging by the look on my son's face, she hasn't yet." His gaze went to the terrace. St. Ives was descending the steps two at a time.

145

"Still can't find Sylvie anywhere." St. Ives strode up to them. "She doesn't—" His gaze snapped to Hubert. "What the devil are you doing here?"

"Your wife sent for me."

"That's ridiculous. She doesn't even like you."

"Nevertheless."

"Well, that makes it even odder that she's gone. She doesn't appear to have taken anything with her, but she's not anywhere to be found. It's not like her. That is"—St. Ives's brows drew together—"She does go off sometimes, but not in the country." He glanced at the others, then frowned round the lawn. "Where's Carfax?"

"Apparently he's missing too," Kitty said in an admirably cool voice. "And no, my mind is not going in the direction scandalmongers would take that. And I'd suggest you avoid following those thoughts as well."

"You can't—" St. Ives choked. "It can't be coincidence."

"Coincidences do happen, but I agree it strains belief. However, I suspect the explanation is more complicated than the easiest assumptions."

"You think they've gone off on a mission?" St. Ives still seemed to have trouble saying the word. "Where?"

"One of the footmen is missing as well," Désirée said. She cast an eye on Hubert as she said it. If Alfred Higgins happened to be one of his agents, he didn't betray it.

"Surely you don't think that has anything to do with Sylvie and Carfax?" St. Ives said.

"I'd never discount anyone, of any station," Désirée said.

"Yes, but Sylvie wouldn't—"

St. Ives broke off. Because Sylvie herself was crossing the lawn from the stables, followed by Julien.

St. Ives moved to meet his wife. "Where the devil have you been?"

"Surely you don't expect me to live in your pocket at this point, St. Ives."

"I assume you were with Carfax." St. Ives stared at Julien, who had strolled up to join them.

"Depends on one's definition of 'with,'" Julien said. "I caught up with Sylvie, who was meeting with her cousin."

"Sylvie doesn't have a cousin within miles of here."

"As a matter of fact, her cousin is employed here. Or was. I don't think he intends to return. I'm sorry, Désirée."

"I take it Alfred Higgins is your cousin?" Désirée said to Sylvie.

Sylvie didn't flinch away or try to dissemble. She knew when it was wasting time to deny something, Désirée would give her that. "That's not his real name. But yes."

"And I assume he was in our household to spy on us?"

"We had reason to think the duke had information here that would be of use." Sylvie turned her gaze to Hubert, who had been standing by in what for him must be unusual silence. "I need to talk to you."

"We're both guests of Mademoiselle Clairineau and Bamford."

"By all means," Désirée said. "There's nothing more disagreeable than having a private conversation in front of others."

"I take it Alfred Higgins is connected to Sylvie's other cousin who was killed because I exposed the list of Royalist agents," Désirée said when Sylvie and Hubert had gone into the salon and St. Ives had stalked off.

"Brothers, I believe," Julien said. "Alfred Higgins's real name was Louis Germont. Several of us tangled with him a few years ago."

Mélanie sucked in her breath. "Good god. You'd think I'd have recognized him. I tended him when he was wounded."

"He had dyed hair and a fairly good disguise," Julien said. "But I confess I had the same thought when I realized who he was." He looked at the others. "Germont was an agent for Fouché. His brother was a Royalist agent. But Fouché collaborated with the Royalists more than once."

"He tried to have me killed because of it," Désirée said. "The night I met Tony."

"Germont got himself hired here to try to uncover evidence against Désirée?" Tony's arm tightened round her shoulders.

"And now has Tony's and my letters." Thank god she had long ago mastered the knack of keeping her voice steady. And really, they'd been in worse predicaments.

"No," Julien said. "I'm quite sure he doesn't have the letters. He slipped off because he knew the staff would be scrutinized and he was afraid he'd be discovered. And also I think because he was afraid Mélanie and I would see through his disguise. Sylvie went to meet him at an inn in the village and give him money to get to London. I managed to overhear half their conversation and then confronted them and got the rest. They agreed to talk in exchange for my helping getting Germont on the stage to London. Germont admitted to getting himself hired here to search for the evidence linking Désirée to his brother's death. But he said it wasn't the first time he'd been to Sawden."

"Let me guess," Désirée said. "He followed me here and tried to kill Tony and me ten years ago."

"Fouché was afraid you knew too much and were talking to Tony. Among other things, you knew Sylvie was dealing with Fouché. Which wasn't good for either of them. Especially since Fouché had been dealing with Uncle Hubert not long before and the two of them had been using Sylvie and Germont to pass information."

"Which I came to warn Tony about on that trip. That Fouché tried to have us killed doesn't surprise me. That Germont managed to follow me does."

"He's obviously brilliant," Tony said.

"Or I was too focused on getting to you."

"I hope you'll all forgive my facilitating his escape," Julien said. "I think we got what we could from him. I'm quite sure he doesn't know where the papers are any more than Sylvie does. And better to have him gone from Sawden."

"Quite," Tony said. "Especially with the papers still missing. And your uncle Hubert now here."

"Sylvie can't tell him anything about us he doesn't know already," Désirée said.

"No," Tony agreed. "But if she could manage to hand him the papers, that would be a different story."

CHAPTER 25

*S*ylvie surveyed Hubert across the small sitting room off the salon that had been the duchess's writing room. It was a surprisingly long time since she'd been alone with her former spymaster. "Well. I didn't think this would work."

"It nearly didn't," Hubert said. "Simon and David are due to arrive this afternoon and I'm missing time with my grandchildren. But I confess you intrigued me. Anything that got you even to speak to me has to be important."

Sylvie folded her arms over the frogged clasps on her spencer. "I think we both have an interest in treason, don't you?"

"Treason to whom? Or perhaps I should say, which country?"

"Whatever else you are, Hubert, you're an Englishman."

Hubert tugged his spectacle frame in that maddening way he did. "I can't change where I was born. But you aren't an Englishwoman."

Sylvie's blue eyes narrowed. "No. But I know how to name an enemy."

"I thought that was what you considered me."

"I did. I do. But sometimes a mutual enemy can make allies."

"A mutual enemy?"

"She destroyed my cousin. And worked to destroy Britain."

"Which isn't your country," Hubert said. "As you just said and have frequently reminded me."

"That's not the part that matters to me. But I assume it matters to you. Our ends may be different, but I think we can agree about the need to act."

Hubert tugged his other ear piece. "And that's enough to make you work with me?"

"Surely you of all people understand working with an enemy, Hubert."

"So I do. And also stabbing them in the back."

Sylvie's brows drew together. "How on earth would I stab you in the back over this?"

"That's what I'm trying to work out."

"You never trusted Bamford."

"That's not entirely true. But I did have questions. More than I do now, actually."

"You have fewer questions now he's living with a French agent?"

"Because he is living with her. Openly. And she isn't in France."

"That doesn't mean she isn't an agent."

"No, I imagine like the rest of us she and Bamford will always be agents, to some degree."

"Well, then. Surely you want to put them in check."

"My dear Sylvie. Why on earth do you think I would waste time putting two people in check who are trying to retire from the game and seem more interested in raising their child than causing trouble for Britain?"

"Because they're the enemy."

"Define enemy."

"Oh, Hubert. You used to be better than this. You can't tell me you put me through everything you did without seeing a clear enemy."

"I saw a clear objective, which isn't quite the same thing."

"And you don't see an objective in taking down Désirée Clairineau?"

Hubert pulled his glasses off and wiped the lenses with his handkerchief. "To be quite honest, I don't."

Sylvie folded her arms. "I don't know what's happened to everyone. Julien was bad enough, but now you've lost your edge as well. This means I don't have any choice."

"Any choice about what?" Hubert settled the spectacles back over his ears.

"Any choice but to find the papers. Then you won't have any choice but to take action."

Raoul and Laura found Franz Stroheim in the drawing room with Lisette and her sister Minette, and the children. The lottery tickets game had given way to charades.

"Are you still looking for clues in the folly?" Colin asked in a break in the game. "When can we play outside again?"

"Soon, I should think," Raoul said.

"I don't suppose you can play with us?" Emily said. The children were all accustomed to the disruptive rhythms of an investigation.

"I can." Laura scooped up Clara, who had toddled over to her.

"And perhaps I can in a bit," Raoul said. "I was hoping for a word with Stroheim."

Stroheim met Raoul's gaze for a moment, then got to his feet with easy assurance. Raoul doubted anyone but a fellow agent would have noticed the wary tension beneath.

They moved into an adjoining sitting room. Sunlight streamed through the windows and dappled the brown and cream striped silk wall hangings. A world away from the shadowy taverns where they had met with Tony when they were plotting to get Barton and St. Georges out of the Conciergerie after Waterloo.

Raoul pushed the door to behind them. "My compliments. How did you work out the location of the secret compartment?"

Franz met his gaze not with surprise so much as recognition of a reckoning overdue. "You must be disappointed."

"On the contrary. As one agent to another, I quite admire your skill." Raoul set his shoulders against the wall and crossed his legs at the ankle. "How did you realize where the papers were?"

"The painting." Stroheim scraped a hand over his head. "The one of the Civil War Lady St. Ives on the stairwell. At least, I assume it's she. The clothes look right. She's wearing a ring with a griffin with a Tudor rose in its teeth. Not the official Southcott crest, so something of hers. The same symbol is scratched on the stone in the passage. Crudely, but you can tell it's the same design."

"Yes." Raoul nodded. "I noticed that today. But then I already knew where the panel was."

"You could have pieced it together if you'd gone looking for the jewels. Any of the agents here might have done."

"Possibly. But you were very enterprising."

"What gave me away?"

"You were wearing a distinctive waistcoat last night. I found a few threads that had scraped off on the stone."

Stroheim shook his head. "Undone by fashion. And to think I just pulled on a waistcoat last night without even paying attention to the pattern."

"It's the small details that catch one." Raoul shifted his shoulders against the wall behind him. "How did you know Tony had papers hidden with the jewels?"

"Tony admitted to me that he'd saved letters from Désirée and copies of letters he wrote to her. One night in London last month, when we were drinking port and I confided more than I should have done about Lisette, and he did the same about Désirée. He told me he was sure the papers were safe. But ever since then, I've been worried. For reasons you may not understand."

"Not fully," Raoul said. "But I'm beginning to piece together an outline."

"Somehow when they were talking about the Southcott jewels last night, I knew," Stroheim said. "Or at least, I guessed. That Tony had hidden the papers with the jewels, and it seemed likely the hiding place was in the passage. I couldn't sleep well, in any case—for a number of reasons. So once the house was quiet, I went into the library and found the passage. From there, it was just a matter of working out where there might be a secret compartment in the passage."

"Just," Raoul said.

Stroheim shrugged. "I've always been good at working out puzzles. It drove my brothers and sisters mad playing games when were children." He glanced towards the door to the drawing room where the charades game was in progress, then looked back at Raoul. "I'm not proud of myself. But I'd do it again."

"My dear boy. If I could tell you how many times I've said the same."

CHAPTER 26

July 1816
Normandy

"Think, Franz." Désirée put her hands on her nephew's shoulders.

"My god." Franz jerked away from her hold. "Do you imagine I ever do anything but think? Do you imagine I'm doing any of this lightly?"

"Of course not." Désirée looked at him across the candlelit sitting room in the cottage that was now her home. The cottage Tony had brought her to that first night, when she'd been bent on stealing back papers from him. As they had both stolen information from each other so many times through the years. "I know you care, and care desperately. I admire you for it, even if it's something I'd never manage myself."

"No?" His gaze skimmed over her face.

"It was harder for me to survive. I've had to learn to be far seeing. I've learnt to live with the consequences. So I know what you do now will have implications years into the future."

"That's rather the idea."

"Implications beyond the ones you're seeing now. Emotions can create challenges for an agent."

Franz held her gaze in the shifting shadows. "Are you saying you've avoided them?"

She laughed, the past cascading over her. "I don't think I could. You've seen enough of my life. You see the life I'm living now." She glanced at the basket in a corner of the cottage sitting room, where Sophie was asleep. "So I know the risks. Tony's risked things for me. Risked his whole life for me, really. I don't want him ever to hate me for it."

"I won't let this come between you and Tony."

"That's not what I meant. I can handle my relationship with Tony. You have to think of what this could do to you and Lisette. If she knew, I think she'd be as worried about what this could do to your relationship as I am about what Tony's actions could do to his feelings for me."

"I can't imagine Tony hating you. I can't imagine him doing anything but loving you."

Désirée smiled at him and shook her head. "That's because you're young. And almost as much of a romantic as Tony is."

"I couldn't hate Lisette. And in any case, I'm not just doing it to protect her. You know how I feel about Metternich. How much longer can I go on like I was, and stay silent?"

For a moment, Désirée saw the ten-year-old Franz who'd come home with a black eye after standing up to a bully. "I can understand that."

He picked up his wineglass from the table where they'd been sitting and took a drink. "You're happy now. You've got past it. You and Tony."

"I don't think one ever really gets past it." Désirée picked up her own glass and turned the stem between her fingers. "We're not actively opposed to each other. We've both found other priorities. But we'll never precisely be allies in every sense. One never quite knows what situation one might face. We're both old enough to understand that."

Franz held her gaze, his own taut. "So you'll take the papers? And get them to where they'll do the most good?"

She tossed down a swallow of wine. As supple as the bottle Tony had opened that first night. Right before she tossed the retrieved papers in the fire. "Was that ever really in doubt?"

He drew in and released his breath, his gaze not leaving her face. "I don't want it to make problems between you and Tony."

"Let me handle that." She set her glass down. The wine glowed blood red in the light from the brace of candles on the table. "I couldn't forgive myself if I didn't help friends in need. And Tony wouldn't love me if I changed because of him."

"But—"

She closed the distance between them again and squeezed his shoulders. "I'll manage, Franz. I have done for a very long time. And Tony and I have to learn to confront challenges. We were going to face something like this sooner or later."

"This doesn't have to be the moment that causes it."

"Perhaps it's as well we go through it now. When I can help friends."

CHAPTER 27

June 1821
Sawden Park, Surrey

Franz Stroheim stood by the back wall of the salon. Not trying to hide from the sunlight streaming in through the French windows or from the gazes of the assembled company. Mélanie and Malcolm, Raoul and Laura, Julien and Kitty, Cordy and Harry. And of course Tony and Désirée. And Lisette. A gathering of former agents. Only Sylvie, Hubert, and Rosalind were absent when it came to former—or present—agents among the house party. Mélanie, seated beside Malcolm on the settee, knew they were observers to this particular drama. Still, it touched on all of them. And the fear of those days of the White Terror, not so very long ago.

"You know what it was like," Franz said. "People were being arrested all round us. People we'd known all our lives. People whose only crime was to fight for their country." He looked at Tony. "We never really talked about what we were doing. When we were working together to save Barton and St. Georges. I mean, we talked about the people we were trying to save, but we didn't talk about it in the larger sense. Yet it was clear friendships came before any nonsense about our countries."

Tony inclined his head. He was sitting on another settee with Désirée. "Cogently put."

"I knew what Lisette risked after Waterloo. I couldn't sleep most nights."

Lisette, sitting on a sofa with Raoul and Laura, drew a breath. "I told you—"

"I know what you said." Franz looked at her, gaze at once tender and uncompromising. "Of course you'd try to make me feel better. But I knew the danger you were in. And not just you. Not just Gaultier Barton. People who'd been my allies only months before. People who wanted what they saw as best for their country. And given what we were seeing from the Bourbons, it was hard to argue they'd been wrong in their allegiance." He sucked in his breath and scraped a hand over his hair. "It was almost a year after the rescue of Barton and St. Georges. Tony and I were dining in a tavern. A hot night. Tony went to get another bottle of wine. His coat was over a chair back. I saw the papers in his pocket. I guessed what they might be. So I grabbed them."

"Wise to learn to seize initiative," Tony said in the same steady voice. "And you gave them to Désirée."

"I made copies. I gave them to Lisette first. So she could protect herself from Royalist agents. But I knew there'd be others in need of protection. So I gave a copy to Désirée too."

"And you let me think you'd taken them." Tony looked at Désirée.

Désirée turned her head to look at him, ringlets and moonstone earrings swinging beside her face. "Well, you assumed as much. And I might have done, given the chance. No sense in causing difficulties between you and Franz. Besides, it didn't break us."

"No." Tony held her gaze for a long moment. "It didn't."

"And so, all in all, it seemed better."

"It was a sacrifice," Franz said. "I shouldn't have let you do it." He looked at Tony. "I'm sorry."

"You were protecting your people."

"Lisette's people. But you and I were allies."

"Surely at this point you've learnt allies can betray allies. What else have the past twenty years taught us? If I could tell you how many times Désirée and I betrayed each other—"

"You and Désirée knew you were on opposite sides."

"Surely you don't think it's only those on opposite sides who'll use information for their own advantage."

"So anything's justified?"

"By no means. I don't lightly betray anyone. Though I have committed far more betrayals than is good for my conscience. I've betrayed the woman I love. But I always made a calculation about the risks and rewards. I can't say I'd make the same calculation if I faced the situation again. But it was not without thought. And I do you the credit of thinking it wasn't without thought for you either."

"No. It wasn't. And I'd probably do it again."

"After what I saw during the White Terror, I might help you."

"I'd never have asked you," Lisette said to Franz. "But I can't deny I'm grateful. On at least one occasion, it may have saved my life. And it certainly saved the lives of others."

"The truth is I felt I needed to do something," Franz said. "Needed to strike a blow. Needed to prove I wasn't Metternich's puppet."

"I don't think you were ever anyone's puppet, Stroheim," Tony said.

"Too often I did his bidding. One has to, as a diplomat. It's the job. To argue one's country's positions. Didn't you ever feel like Castlereagh's puppet? Or at least Britain's?"

"I wouldn't have put it that way. But I suppose so. It's one reason I'm not a diplomat anymore."

"And the reason I'm leaving the diplomatic service."

"Franz." Lisette cast a quick glance at him.

Stroheim met her gaze. "Surely you realized long since I couldn't go back, beloved. There's no place left for me. The patchy ground I managed to stand on during the Congress has crumbled to bits. Even my father understands that. He may not be happy, but he wouldn't force me into a life that would make me miserable. In truth, I think it's begun to make him miserable as well."

"Your father has always been an insightful man," Désirée said. "And a generous one. I hope he finds happiness himself."

Stroheim met her gaze for a moment. "When I left, he said he looked forward to visiting me. He understood I wouldn't be coming back. In truth, I don't think he wanted me to." He looked round the company. "Because the truth is I wasn't just helping Désirée and Sophie escape. I was escaping myself. My father understood that."

"Escaping doesn't mean you can't go back," Lisette said in quiet voice.

"Perhaps one day. To visit. Your life is here now. Your family are here. I can't see you living anywhere else."

"No. Maybe. That doesn't mean—"

"Doesn't it?"

Lisette's gaze caught his own. Their future teetered between them. Damnable they had to settle this in front of others. And yet perhaps inevitable, given the intertwined complications of their lives.

"You'll always have a place here," Tony said. "For that matter, you'll always have family here. Désirée will be far happier not being alone with my side of the family."

Désirée laughed. "I'd manage. But yet—"

"We're all finding new things to do with ourselves," Raoul said. "You have a lot of options, Stroheim."

"I know," Stroheim said. "I'm happier than I've been in years. Since I entered the diplomatic service, if it comes to that. Love may not define one. But it can rescue one."

Tony slid his arm round Désirée. "I know all about that."

Stroheim looked from Désirée to Tony. "I never meant to make trouble for you, though."

"You didn't," Désirée said. "I made my own choices, as I always do. As I always have."

"Why do you think I fell in love with her?" Tony said.

"We were going to confront something of the sort at some point after we decided to be together," Désirée said.

"Still. I didn't have to push it."

"We got through it," Tony said. "There are always things to get through. As you will discover." His gaze flickered to Lisette. "Both of you."

CHAPTER 28

"*Y*ou have to let me tell him." Franz slammed the cottage door shut and strode across the tile floor.

"For god's sake, Franz." Désirée shifted Sophie on her hip. "That will just make it harder for the two of you to work together."

"But I can't stand by while he blames you—"

Désirée smoothed a strand of Sophie's hair that was standing up. "He blames me for sharing the documents. Which I did."

"But you didn't steal them from him."

"No. Not this time. But I've done worse in the past."

"But not since you've been"—Franz drew in and released his breath—"what you are now."

"Living in a fairy tale, you mean?" She pressed a kiss to Sophie's forehead. "We're never going to be able to continue this improbable life we've begun if we can't get past the inevitable betrayals."

"You think betrayal is inevitable?"

"I think clashing viewpoints are inevitable." Désirée gently detached Sophie's fingers from her pearls. "I think interests and loyalties that tug us in different directions are inevitable. We can't hide from it. We can't pretend those tensions don't exist. I'm happy in the country, raising our child. But we'll never endure if that's all I am. I'll go mad. And I won't be the woman he fell in love with."

"And you think you can endure if—"

"He thinks I betrayed him? I hope so."

"You're testing him."

Désirée looked down at her and Tony's child and then leant her cheek against Sophie's head. "Perhaps I'm testing both of us."

CHAPTER 29

June 1821
Sawden Park, Surrey

*H*ubert met Raoul in the hall outside the salon. "O'Roarke. Have you seen Bamford? Time I was taking my leave."

Raoul scanned his former rival's face. "Got what you came for?"

"As it happens, I don't think there was much to come for." Hubert pushed his spectacles up on his nose. "Not surprising, really. Sylvie has some odd starts. I needed to see what she was up to, but I didn't expect it to come to much. You might mention that to Bamford and Mademoiselle Clairineau."

"I will. I imagine they will find it reassuring."

Hubert nodded, then hesitated a moment. His gaze flickered over Raoul's face. "You look well."

"Thank you. I'm still a bit stiff. But close to being back to my old self."

Hubert regarded him, hands jammed in his pockets. "I was worried."

Raoul returned his gaze. "Mélanie told me you came to Berkeley Square the night I was wounded. It's appreciated."

Hubert grunted. "You make life more interesting, O'Roarke. I should probably be relieved you aren't going to be stirring unrest in Spain. But I confess I'm—"

"Concerned about the unrest I'll be stirring at home?"

Hubert gave what with him passed for a grin. "I should be. Though I enjoy you as an opponent. But I was thinking more of what it means to leave the field. I was younger than you when I did. Coming into the title, I couldn't live the same life I had. Or so it seemed. Bamford managed to defy the strictures of his position, but I didn't try to that degree. Amelia seemed to appreciate having me at home. Not that it—" He grimaced, tugged off his spectacles, pushed them back on his nose. "Enjoy your time with your family. It's a foundation you'll need later. Without it, you can find yourself—lacking."

Raoul nodded. There was a time he'd never had thought to feel sympathy for Hubert Mallinson. A lot had changed. "Sometimes it's hard, in the midst of the needs of the moment, to sort out what truly matters. Or what matters most from a host of things that matter. Without Malcolm, I'm not sure I'd have been able to do so."

"I've frequently bemoaned Malcolm's tendency to see the human side of the equation. But I confess at times it has its uses." Hubert pushed at his spectacles again, though they didn't seem to have moved an inch. "Now, for god's sake, help me find Bamford before I make a complete fool of myself."

∽

HUBERT SHOOK Tony's hand before the gleaming front door. "Thank you for your hospitality. It's been an illuminating visit. My felicitations to you both." He bowed to Désirée, who was standing beside Tony in the entrance hall. "And to you and Mr. Wilcox." He inclined his head to Hetty, who had also come to see him off, as had Mélanie, Malcolm, Julien, Kitty, Laura, Raoul, Harry, and Cordelia.

"Thank you, Hubert," Hetty said. "Do give Amelia my regards."

"Love to David and Simon," Julien said.

"And Aunt Amelia and Lucinda." Kitty kissed Hubert's cheek. "Hug the children for us."

"Safe travels," Mélanie said. It was an odd thing to be saying to Hubert, but felt quite natural.

Hubert nodded. "You should stop on your way back to town." His gaze moved to Malcolm and Raoul. "All of you."

"Thank you," Raoul said. He was always easier with Hubert than Malcolm was.

"We'd like to see you," Malcolm said. "All of you."

Hubert nodded and went out the door with a smile that looked genuine. And just possibly might have been so.

"Do you think that's it?" Kitty said when the door closed. "He'll let the matter go?"

"He more or less told me he would," Raoul said. "And asked me to tell Tony and Désirée."

A light step sounded on the stairs. Sylvie came down the stairs, attired in a fresh blue-sprigged muslin, hair arranged in artless loose curls, and looked from the door to the assembled crowd. "So that's it?" she said. "All neatly tidied away, no consequences? I should have known ducal power would win out in the end."

Julien turned to regard her, arms folded. "There's one thing I don't understand. Who did you have write the notes? And why send them with so much else going on?"

Sylvie raised a penciled brow. "What notes?"

Julien returned her stare. "You know, I almost believe you. It always seemed a bit overly dramatic for you."

"Someone sent you notes?" Sylvie asked. "What sort of notes?"

"Not just him," Raoul said.

"You intrigue me." Sylvie's gaze scanned the group. "But I don't see what I'd have had to gain—"

She broke off as a streak of gray ran out of the drawing room with Colin, Sophie, Emily, and Jessica in close pursuit.

"Drop it," Colin called.

Mélanie bent to grab Berowne, who skittered past her. "Does he have a mouse?"

"No, it's a piece of paper." Colin pounced on Berowne, who had knocked the paper under the console table and was trying to bat it out. He grabbed Berowne by the back of his neck and scooped him up. Emily snatched up the paper.

"It fell out of Lady Rosalind's reticule," Jessica said.

"She left it on a chair," Sophie added. "The reticule. Berowne knocked it on the floor and the paper fell out."

Laura took the paper from Emily and unfolded it.

"Let me guess," Tony said. "Another note?"

Laura nodded and held the paper out to him. "I'm not sure whom it was intended for. But it's definitely in the same vein as the others."

"Oh, for heaven's sake." Rosalind appeared in the drawing room doorway. "Didn't any of you guess? Why does everyone think Sylvie is the only one in this family capable of duplicity?"

CHAPTER 30

"I don't think anyone would suggest that." Tony folded the note and regarded his daughter. "Perhaps we should go into the salon."

Rosalind met her father's gaze and inclined her head. Tony glanced round the others as they started to edge away. "All of us," he said. "It's time for answers." He looked at Colin, Emily, Jessica, and Sophie. "Thank you. You've been very helpful."

The children nodded. Sophie, Mélanie noted, already had the same look Colin, Jessica, and Emily often did. It must be inherent in children of spies. Piecing together bits of information and accepting that one didn't have all the answers. Though the look Colin gave her over Berowne's head said he would ask questions later.

They settled themselves in the salon, most of them drawn back a bit, as they had been before. But Rosalind didn't seem to mind the audience. In fact, Mélanie sensed she relished it. She looked at her father with the air of one who has wanted to say something for a long time.

"I suppose you're wondering why I did it. I suppose everyone is, but you especially, Papa. Though I should think it was obvious.

I was born to be a princess. And I quite liked it for a while. But it was easy. I never had to work at it. And no one ever really seemed to appreciate it. At least, you didn't."

"I've always been proud of you, Rosy." Tony's gaze was steady on his youngest daughter's face.

"Oh, you were an attentive enough father. More than a lot of my friends' parents. I'll give you that. You paid attention to us when you were home and you genuinely did seem interested. But you can't tell me we were that central. That you were anything like as interested in us as you are in her daughter." She glanced towards Désirée, who had taken a seat off to the side, then towards the front of the house and the drawing room, to which the children had returned. "Sophie is very engaging. I like her. But she certainly caught your interest as I never did. It's quite obvious what it takes to catch your interest. You like being a spy better than being a duke. And you like spies better than aristocrats."

"Rosy, you never had to be different to get my attention. You must know I always loved you as you are."

"You have to admit your attention was focused outside of England, Papa."

"If you're saying you did all this merely—"

"Merely to get your attention? Oh no. I wasn't even particularly aware of wanting your attention. I did it because I realized I agreed with you. It's agreeable being a princess and having people pay one court. Mama knows that." She cast a quick glance at Hetty. "But it's much more interesting wielding power oneself. And while I'd never want not to reign in the beau monde, it's more exciting moving among agents. I quite understand why you were gone so much. But I also understand about preserving a veneer. Honestly, you couldn't do that yourself? After you'd given up so much to lead a life of adventure, you had to give it all up for love in a cottage?"

"I'm sorry, Rosy. But what drew me to being an agent wasn't what drew you."

"Really? You were clearly bored by life in the beau monde. You think I wasn't? I was quite young when I realized what you were really doing. All it took was overhearing one or two comments and finding one or two pieces of code for me to begin to piece it together. I was terribly impressed. My dull father was actually something quite exciting."

"When in fact I was dull after all."

"Oh no. You were genuinely fascinating. Oh, don't get me wrong. You didn't betray so much of what you were doing that I knew details. But I saw enough. Especially when I went to the Peninsula with you. I saw how one could move through the beau monde and all the while live a different life behind it. Like those scenes behind the gauzy curtain at the theatre that only show up when they shine a light through it. I saw Gaspar stealing papers the night we met. That's what caught my attention." Her brows drew together. "It was only later that it occurred to me that if he'd been a rather better agent, I wouldn't have realized he was one at all so quickly."

"Always fatal," Julien murmured. He was leaning against the silk-hung wall, legs crossed at the ankle.

Rosalind regarded him for a moment. "I wish I'd met you in the Peninsula."

"You did," Julien said. "I looked down my nose at you on the sidelines at a regimental ball, gossiping with the dowagers. And we danced together at Charles Stuart's. I was wearing a uniform of the 95th."

Rosalind folded her arms. "Quite proving my point. Gaspar wasn't nearly clever enough. Though at least he had the wit to see that I was better at the game than he was, and to appreciate my efforts. A lot of husbands would simply try to keep their wives out of it. Even if their wives were cleverer than they were."

"Especially if they were cleverer," Julien said.

Rosalind looked at her mother. "You told me I'd appreciate my freedom when I married. And I did. But it wasn't being married."

She wrinkled her nose. "Except that being married gave me the freedom to be an agent properly. Or at least better than I could before." She turned to Désirée. "I envy you. You didn't have to play the beau monde game. I mean, I'd have missed it, but it also means you could be an agent from the start."

"I'm not precisely sure what 'the start' is," Désirée said. "But it did let me be an agent when I wanted to. I couldn't see another reasonable way to achieve what I wanted in life."

"I suppose I could say the same. Though I didn't care about the politics of it as much as you did. And then it turned out Gaspar was more interested in his friends than in me. Which made things simpler, all things considered."

"It can," Julien said, with a steady gaze that was not without sympathy. "Though it can also be frustrating."

Rosalind shrugged. "Better than having him hover over me. Very agreeable to be given my freedom. And at least we have the same goals. He may not be the most able agent, but he's quite good at backup. Easier, in some ways, to have someone one can have a rational conversation with. Not everything is a deathless romance." She looked from her mother to her father and Désirée. "Not that I don't understand the impulse to indulge. Even when it isn't part of the mission. But how could you so lose sight of what matters as to upend your whole life for *that*?"

"Perhaps because we realized what matters." It was the duchess who spoke.

"What? What you laughingly call love? Which surely, at this point, we can all admit—the children are out of earshot, after all—there's no chance will last more than the length of a mission or the impulse of the moment." Rosalind's gaze moved to Julien. "I don't understand you at all. You were brilliant. I can understand wanting the title, but why give up so much?"

Julien leant back against the wall. "I don't believe I've given up anything."

"Sylvie thinks you have." Rosalind looked at her sister-in-law.

Julien shot a look at Sylvie as well. "Sylvie and I don't agree about a lot of things."

"And you." Rosalind's gaze moved to Raoul. "You were a name to be feared. And now you seem to be focused on dandling children. While you." She turned to Mélanie. "You didn't even hold on to reigning over the beau monde." Her gaze shifted to Désirée. "You're the worst of all, perhaps. I was sure you were hiding something, but from what I can tell, you haven't done anything remotely interesting since Waterloo."

"Define interesting," Désirée said. "But by your definition, you may be right."

"You can't want this," Rosalind said. "Even if Papa's bewitched by the romantic haze, you can't tell me you are so lost to sense. Ever since I learnt you were in England, I've been trying to make out what you really wanted."

Désirée got to her feet, moved to Tony's side, and slid her hand through his arm. "Your father."

"She'll never believe that," Tony said.

Rosalind's gaze flickered. "You're right," she said. But there was just the faintest note of uncertainty in her voice.

"We made a grave error," Hetty said. "We didn't give you the least idea of what is really important in life. Because we didn't have the least idea ourselves. I am so sorry, my darling."

"Don't be." Rosalind straightened her shoulders and tossed her hair back. "I quite like my life. I just couldn't bear to sit back and watch you all be so foolish with yours. Silly of me to try to jolt you to your senses, perhaps. But one has to find some way to amuse oneself in the country."

CHAPTER 31

$\mathcal{T}$ony looked out from the terrace across the lawn where the children were once again playing round the folly. "I always knew I'd failed at a great deal. I just didn't realize how much until today. Or how close to home it cut."

Désirée slid her arm round him. "I don't think one can get to our age without feeling one has failed at a number of things. But Rosalind is very much your daughter."

"Is that supposed to comfort me or horrify me?"

Désirée smiled up at the man she loved. "It means she has a great deal to sort out in life. And the resources to do so."

"I hope so." Tony pressed his lips to her hair, then looked at Franz and Lisette, who were crossing the lawn hand in hand to join the children. "You were kind. Five years ago when Stroheim took the papers."

"Rot. I'm never kind."

"You didn't want to create complications for Franz."

Désirée leant against Tony and watched Franz pause and lift Lisette's hand to his lips. "He was coping with enough. I admired him for taking a stand. He helped people we both cared about. It would hardly have improved the situation if you'd turned on him."

"Who's to say I would have done?"

"You were angry enough at me when you thought I'd taken the list of Royalists."

"But I got over it. Of course, I wasn't in love with Stroheim. Which also made the betrayal cut harder."

"But we had to get used to that."

"Did we?"

She glanced across the lawn at the light dancing through the tangle of birch and larch trees, picking out myriad shades of green, but not revealing half of what was hidden in the shadows. "Something was going to come up. At some point. That would pull us in opposite directions."

"Not necessarily."

Désirée pressed her head against his shoulder. "My eternal romantic."

"What about you?"

"What about me?"

"Worrying about young lovers."

"Mmm." She tilted her head back. "That doesn't sound like me."

"That sounds very like you. You just wouldn't admit it."

"A crisis would hit them harder than us. We know how to weather it. They can handle a lot, though." She watched Franz and Lisette, now in the folly, kneeling down to talk to Sophie and Jessica. "I'm impressed with both of them."

"So am I."

"And I confess a part of me likes the idea—"

"What?"

Désirée turned her gaze back to Tony. "I love that we found what we have when we did. But the idea of finding it young."

A smile lit his eyes. "You were absurdly young."

"When we met. But when we decided to be together"—her mouth twisted—"at the risk of sounding maudlin, when we committed to each other, we'd been through almost two decades. We never tumbled into young love. I don't think the Rannochs did either, young as they were. But for all Franz and Lisette have been through, there's something very young about their feelings. I don't think either has loved before. Not like this. I remember them at Malmaison, looking as though they were on a balcony in Verona. My heart was in my throat, thinking of what might lie ahead. That they've managed to preserve that feeling this long says a lot. I'd like them to hold on to it."

Tony smiled. "You were maternal long before you had Sophie."

"Possibly."

"And an incurable romantic."

"Because I lied to you?"

"Because you risked what we had to protect someone else's romance."

"I told you. I knew we were going to have to face the risk."

"You were testing me."

"I was testing us."

"Because you didn't trust that my feelings for you would last. Haven't you realized yet?"

"Realized what?"

He kissed her, heedless of who might be watching. "That I'll love you no matter what."

"I WAS WRONG," Mélanie said. "I was so focused on where the next threat would come from. But I never thought of Rosalind."

"That's the thing about threats," Malcolm said. "One never knows where they'll surface."

Mélanie adjusted her hold on Berowne's lead. She and Malcolm had taken him for a ramble over the lawn. She could hear the children's shouts of glee from the folly interspersed by barks from the dogs. A new game was in progress, a mock tournament. All the children had thrown themselves into it with the easy abandon of childhood. They met new friends and accepted them into their circle without question. Even the St. Ives children didn't seem to have grasped the social distinctions that were so important to their parents.

Berowne had stopped to sniff something in the grass. Mélanie paused to let him explore, and perched on a stone wall that bordered a raised bed of lavender and larch trees. "So by watching for knives in an alley or assassins in the shrubbery, one can miss subtler cues?" she asked.

"Possibly." Malcolm sat beside her. "Though there still can be assassins in the shrubbery. Sylvie's cousin apparently once tried to kill Désirée and Tony in the folly where our children are playing right now. But we can't live in fear."

"Or forget who we were."

"Rosalind accused us of forgetting." Malcolm turned sideways to look at her. The sunlight fell across his face, dappled by the shadows from the overhanging trees. "Do you miss it?"

"Do I miss what?"

"Everything Rosalind accused us of giving up?"

Mélanie glanced at Berowne, who had rolled onto his back and was batting at the grass. Quite as if he hadn't uncovered a plot a short time before. "We haven't really given it up. That's the whole point."

"No. But it's not the life you'd have had before you married me."

"Thank goodness." Mélanie leant forwards to rub Berowne's stomach, then sat back on the stone wall to look at Malcolm. "We'll never escape a life of intrigue. And to own the truth, I wouldn't want to. I can admit that now. But some of our most exciting adventures are being a family."

DÉSIRÉE LINGERED on the terrace before going in to make sure all was in order for dinner. Tony had gone to join the children in the folly, as had Malcolm and Mélanie and several of the other adults. A mock tournament seemed to have given way to a court ball. Tony was dancing with Sophie, twirling her in the sunlight that shot between the stone pillars. A mock castle meant to conjure memories of a time that never was.

Of course, she could never admit that at nineteen there were times she'd been caught up in the fairy tale herself. The fairy tale where this dashing prince from an enemy country might prove to be her true love. Where she actually believed in true love. Where what was between them might be stronger than any pull between their countries. Nonsense, of course. Not the stuff of the real world. But at nineteen one could escape into those moments. And if she were honest, one could do the same at nine-and-twenty. Or nine-and-thirty. And of course, that was much what she'd done now, at forty-some.

She glanced at Tony again, now bowing to Jessica Rannoch. His eyes still had that light she'd glimpsed across the table in the kitchen of his luxurious "safe cottage" all those years ago. Boyish adventure in a man almost twice her age. She'd thought he was naive and heedless then. In the years since, she'd seen the sharpness of his vision and the depth of his feeling for others. She'd come to appreciate his humanity. But that impulsive recklessness, the urge to rush off into adventure was still there. And no doubt always would be.

And she loved him for it. Désirée turned to the house, then glanced back for one last look at the sunlight glancing off the stone, and the laughing group within the sun-warmed walls. It wasn't a fairy tale. But it might be something better.

SNEAK PEEK AT THE GRESHAM
SCANDAL

Malcolm and Mélanie Suzanne Rannoch's adventures
in espionage and investigation continue
in Tracy Grant's new historical mystery
On sale May 2025

PROLOGUE

April, 1819
Normandy

*T*rees overhung the cottage, making it appear smaller
than it probably was. Creamy yellow stone softened by
vines with a timber roof and wood-framed windows painted a
slate blue. Not the place one would imagine an agent who had
been feared across the Continent hiding from the world. But then
as she had learnt from her Bow Street runner brother's investigations, sometimes the most dangerous people were the most
deceptive.

Harriet Roth hesitated in front of the blue-painted front door.
For all the risks she'd run recently, it seemed absurd to cavil at

this one. Yet at the same time it felt a significant step. A move into the unknown from which she could not return.

She rapped at the door. Light footsteps on a stone floor. The door opened to reveal a tall woman in a moss green gown, brown hair caught up in a disheveled knot, a small girl of about three clinging to her skirt.

"You must be Harriet," the woman said with smile that was quick and disarming. "This is Sophie. And I'm Désirée."

Harriet must have started. Somehow it was a surprise to hear the woman speak the name.

Désirée gave a full-throated laugh. "Did you think I'd use another name? I've used so many through the years. I'm more myself here than I have been anywhere for the past two decades."

Sophie tugged at her mother's skirt. "In a minute, *petite*." Désirée touched her daughter's hair. "We don't have a lot of visitors. She's very excited."

"We made cookies." Sophie stretched out a hand and grasped Harriet's fingers.

"She may want to go up to her room first, *petite*," the woman said.

"It's all right. I can't refuse cookies." The child's smile was infectious and made Harriet miss her nephews Samuel and Dorian. But more than cookies, Harriet was eager for information.

Désirée smiled and took Harriet's valise. Sophie pulled Harriet into a sun-splashed sitting room with dark wood mellowed by age, a huge stone fireplace, and tapestry furniture. A plate of the promised cookies and a pot of coffee sat on a table before a settee strewn with comfortable cushions.

"You had no trouble getting here?" Désirée asked as she poured coffee.

Harriet shook her head and took a cookie from the plate Sophie was holding out. "The carriage met me at the dock. And I made sure they let me off in the woods as instructed."

"Thank you." The woman held out a cup of coffee. "I know the instructions were a bit circuitous. But we find it best to take precautions."

Given her past and the current conditions in France for anyone connected to the Bonaparte regime, it seemed a massive understatement. Harriet accepted the coffee and stirred in milk.

Désirée sat back in a chair, her own coffee cup cradled in one hand. "You're quite daring."

"Not really. Not at all compared to you."

Désirée took a sip of coffee. "I've been doing this for far longer. And I was trained for it."

"You must have started somewhere." Harriet took a bite of cookie and smiled at Sophie in approval. Sophie, halfway through her own cookie, grinned.

"There is that," Désirée acknowledged. "Difficult to remember the start now."

"I may not be an agent," Harriet said. "But I'm no stranger to keeping secrets."

"No. According to our mutual friend you're brilliant at it." Désirée took another sip of coffee. "Are you sure about this?"

Harriet set down her cup. "Why else would I have come all this way?"

"I don't doubt your daring. Or your commitment. I don't doubt the lure of adventure. But there's no shame in facing a risk and deciding to walk away."

"Are you advising me to do that?"

"By no means. But I'm suggesting you consider the risks. I'm a dangerous collaborator."

Harriet sat forward in her chair and met the gaze of the agent who had been feared across the Continent. "Let's get to work."

CHAPTER ONE
September, 1819

RIFLE SHOTS PINGED off the rocks. Mélanie rolled to the dusty ground, wondering how the shooter could have reloaded so fast. The rifle fire echoed again before she could begin to make it to the shelter of trees. She pushed herself up against the hard ground only to come awake and feel smooth linen and a soft pillow beneath her fingers.

She was in her bed, in Berkeley Square, not in the Cantabrian Mountains. But the pinging sound hadn't stopped. Not rifle fire. Gravel thrown at the window.

Before she even turned her head, she knew her husband Malcolm was awake beside her. She exchanged a quick glance with him in the dark, more sense than sight, then grabbed her dressing gown from the foot of the bed and ran to the window.

Malcolm stumbled to the window beside her. They pushed up the sash together. The moonlight glanced off the pale stone of the house and lit the upturned faces of the man and woman who stood beneath the window. The man's unruly shock of dark hair and the woman's tumble of dark gold curls. Jeremy Roth, friend, fellow investigator, and Bow Street runner. And Judith, Malcolm's cousin, and Jeremy's wife of less than a year.

"Come to the front door," Malcolm called.

"Get Raoul and Laura," he said to Mélanie as he struck a flint to a candle.

Malcolm ran down the stairs. Mélanie rapped on the door of Malcolm's father Raoul and his wife Laura. "It's Jeremy and Judith," she called.

Raoul and Laura emerged, wrapped in dressing gowns, with a speed that said they'd heard and had merely been waiting to see if they were needed. In a family of former spies, no one slept soundly. Their gazes flickered across her face.

"I don't know any more," Mélanie said. It was not wholly usual for Jeremy to come to them with a case at unexpected times of day. It was more surprising for Judith to be with him. Though she had been managing to work her way into his investigations with admirable tenacity.

The door creaked open in the hall below. By the time Mélanie, Laura, and Raoul reached the base of the stairs, Malcolm was ushering in Jeremy, greatcoated but bareheaded, and Judith, wrapped in a blue velvet cloak.

"I'm sorry," Jeremy said.

"No need," Malcolm told him. "But why the dramatic arrival?"

"You answer your own door at night," Jeremy said, nodding to Mélanie, Laura, and Raoul. "Admirable, but it occurred to me it makes middle of the night visits complicated. I wasn't sure who ringing the bell would wake and in truth we wanted to keep this quiet."

"I told him picking the lock would be better than throwing gravel," Judith said.

"Not necessarily," Malcolm told his cousin, moving to hold open the library door. "Screams of shock have a way of waking people."

"Oh stuff." Judith moved past him into the library. "Julien used to break into your house all the time. I imagine he still does."

"He has a key actually," Malcolm said. "We'll get you one."

"We don't all have to hear whatever it is," Raoul said from the base of the stairs.

"No," Jeremy said. "We'll need all of you." He turned to face them as they moved into the library and Malcolm lit the lamps by the fireplace. "It's Harriet. She's disappeared."

Mélanie cast a quick glance at Malcolm and then at Laura and Raoul. Harriet was Jeremy's sister, who had lived with him and helped care for his sons when his first wife left him and now continued to live with him and Judith. Quiet, ironic, stylish, she had been on the edges of so many investigations but never at the heart. Not even their investigation into the death of Jeremy's first wife.

"She didn't leave a note?" Mélanie asked.

Jeremy shook his head. He was pacing before the unlit fire-place. "We all had dinner together. Serena woke with a bad dream and Judith and I got up to sit with her. Harriet's door wasn't latched and it swung open. I went to close it and saw she wasn't in her bed." He paused, cheeks flushed in the lamplight. "I wouldn't intrude on my sister's privacy. But when I saw the bed was undisturbed, I glanced in. There was no response when I called her name, so I went in." He hesitated. "In the life we lead, one worries."

"Understandable," Malcolm said, gaze steady on Jeremy's face. Mélanie could feel the echoes of the night Jeremy had summoned Malcolm to the tavern where his first wife lay knifed to death.

Jeremy inclined his head, gaze filled with ghosts. "Her reticule and cloak were gone. Nothing else. From what I can tell from physical evidence, she left the house by the front door."

"Jeremy." Mélanie chose her words carefully. Harriet was a friend, but they were hardly confidantes. "Harriet is a grown woman." Mélanie wasn't sure of Harriet's precise age, but somewhere in her late twenties or early thirties, she suspected. "Could she—"

"I said as much." Judith jumped up from the Queen Anne chair where she'd plopped when they came into the library. "Just because Harriet has devoted her life to Jeremy and the boys doesn't mean she has no other interests. Gentlemen can be so obtuse when it comes to their sisters."

Jeremy's gaze clashed with his wife's. "You know perfectly well Harriet doesn't—"

"That's just it, Jeremy," Judith said to her husband. "We don't know what Harriet does with her spare time. And it's really no concern of ours."

"No—" Jeremy sucked in his breath.

"For a Radical," Judith said, "you're ridiculously old-fashioned about your sister, dearest."

"It's all very well," Jeremy said, "but as we often say however

184

much we may want to change the world, this is the world we live in. And you know what would happen if people realized Harriet—"

"Had a lover?" Judith said. "No one's going to realize it if we don't make a fuss."

"Do you have any reason to believe Harriet was involved with anyone?" Raoul asked in a quiet voice. "While I would not want to intrude on anyone's personal life, I also know better than to assume the obvious for anyone's disappearance."

"No," Jeremy said. "There was never the least hint—"

"Don't be silly, darling," Judith said. "You know perfectly well she'd shut her door for hours on end and she was always scribbling away--"

"All of which anyone may do without having a secret lover," Laura said.

"Well, yes," Judith acknowledged. "But now that she's missing—"

"A point," Malcolm agreed. "But there's more than one reason a person can disappear. And given the attitudes of her family, I find it hard to believe Harriet would elope." He held Jeremy's gaze for a moment. "What did you find in her room?"

Jeremy gave a faint smile that did not reach is eyes. "You know me well enough to know I searched."

"I wouldn't do you the discredit of thinking otherwise."

Jeremy's mouth twisted. "I'm not sure it's to my credit. But the only significant thing I found was this." He reached into his coat and pulled out a rectangular calling card on heavy cream laid paper. He held it out to Malcolm.

Mélanie moved to her husband's side and started at the black print on the card. A name that suggested much and explained nothing. A noted roué. A known Radical. A brilliant composer. A man whose life was cloaked in secrets. The former lover of Jeremy's first wife.

Tristram Gresham.

ACKNOWLEDGMENTS

Every book is challenging in its own way, but this novella was written during an extraordinarily busy time, and I'm particularly grateful for all the help and support. As always, huge thanks to my wonderful agent, Nancy Yost, for her insights and brilliant eye for framing the story and editing cover copy. Thanks to Natanya Wheeler, a fabulous Director of Digital Rights, for shepherding the book expertly through each stage of the publication process. Natanya also designs the covers for the series. For this book, she had the idea of adding a pet on the cover, which inspired me to give Berowne an even larger role in the story than he already had. To Sarah Younger for helping the book along through production and publication, and to Sarah and Christina Miller for superlative social media support. To Hana Muslea for the beautiful character and quote cards. And to the entire team at Nancy Yost Literary Agency for their fabulous work. Their creativity and dedication make all of them a dream to work with. Malcolm, Mélanie, and all the other characters (including Berowne) and I are all very fortunate to have their support.

Thank you to Eve Lynch for the meticulous and thoughtful copyediting. I love sharing the Rannochs with you and so appreciate your care for getting their story right when it comes to everything from historical usage to series continuity.

Thank you to Kristen Loken for a magical author photo. This one is particularly special because we were back in San Francisco's War Memorial Opera House for the Merola Grand Finale. Your brilliance never fails to amaze me, Kristen!

I am very fortunate to have a wonderful group of writer friends near and far who make being a writer less solitary. Thanks in particular to Lauren Willig for sharing the joys of historical research and the challenges of juggling life as a writer and a mom. To Penelope Williamson, for sharing wonderful writer escapes to the Oregon Shakespeare Festival and the Oregon coast, during one of which this novella was finished, and hours of inspiring talk. Thank you to the #momswritersclub for bimonthly chats that are energizing and inspiring, and especially to Shay Galloway, with whom I now co-host the chats, and to Jessica Payne for starting the group and to Jessica and Sara Read for their wonderful #MomsWritersClub YouTube channel on which Mélanie and I had the fun of doing a guest interview.

Thank you to the readers who support Malcolm and Mélanie and their friends and provide wonderful insights on my website and social media, and especially on the Goodreads Discussion Group for the series.

Thanks to Gregory Paris and jim saliba for creating and updating a fabulous website that chronicles Malcolm and Mélanie's adventures.

And thank you to my daughter Mélanie, for brainstorming *The Southcott Jewels* (including where the jewels were hidden), proof-reading, and supporting me all the way through the process, during a particularly busy time in our lives. I am so proud that my website now includes "Mélanie's Corner" for her stories, starting with her wonderful series *Talea's Mysteries*. From the time she could touch the keys, Mélanie has contributed something to each of my books. This is Mélanie's contribution to this story – "I love my mom so much, and I love her books. I hope you like this new addition to The Rannoch Fraser Mysteries. I'm so happy I got to help with it a little too. Love you, Mummy!"

ALSO BY TRACY GRANT

Traditional Regencies

WIDOW'S GAMBIT

FRIVOLOUS PRETENCE

THE COURTING OF PHILIPPA

Lescaut Quartet

DARK ANGEL

SHORES OF DESIRE

SHADOWS OF THE HEART

RIGHTFULLY HIS

The Rannoch Fraser Mysteries

HIS SPANISH BRIDE

LONDON INTERLUDE

VIENNA WALTZ

IMPERIAL SCANDAL

THE PARIS AFFAIR

THE PARIS PLOT

BENEATH A SILENT MOON

THE BERKELEY SQUARE AFFAIR

THE MAYFAIR AFFAIR

INCIDENT IN BERKELEY SQUARE

LONDON GAMBIT

MISSION FOR A QUEEN

GILDED DECEIT

MIDWINTER INTRIGUE

ABOUT THE AUTHOR

Photo by Kristen Loken

Tracy Grant studied British history at Stanford University and received the Firestone Award for Excellence in Research for her honors thesis on shifting conceptions of honor in late-fifteenth-century England. She lives in the San Francisco Bay Area with her young daughter and four cats. In addition to writing, Tracy works for the Merola Opera Program, a professional training program for opera singers, pianists, and stage directors. Her real-life heroine is her daughter Mélanie, who is very cooperative about Mummy's writing time and is starting to write herself. She is currently at work on her next book chronicling the adventures of Malcolm and Mélanie Suzanne Rannoch. Visit her on the web at www.tracygrant.org.

Made in the USA
Las Vegas, NV
07 December 2024

13315995R00115